The Mysteries of Wentworth Manor

The Mysteries of Wentworth Manor

Copyright © 2016 tdr

All rights reserved. No part of this publication may be reproduced, distributed, or transmitted in any form or by any means, including photocopying, recording, or other electronic or mechanical methods, without the prior written permission of the publisher, except in the case of brief quotations embodied in critical reviews and certain other noncommercial uses permitted by copyright law.

ISBN: 9781728916279 (Paperback)

Editor: T. M. Mettam

Editor: D. Mettam

Any references to historical events, real people, or real places are used fictitiously. Names, characters, and places are products of the author's imagination.

Independently Published

First printing edition September 2016.

First Edition ISBN: 9781539022152 (Paperback)

Second Printing Edition October 2018

For Gloria

Thank you for always sharing my dream.

I love you; continue to rest well.

For RAR, TMM, and SDR

My world would not be the same without you in it. All my love, ladies.

And for THS.

Thank you for opening my eyes.

I love you, Always.

Chapter 1

The darkness enveloped the forest quickly. A light mist washed over the large area and Bailey shivered in the chill of the night air.

"What am I doing here, again?" she wondered aloud. Chuckling to herself at the sudden burst of fear that enveloped her, she took a three hundred and sixty degree turn. "Looks just like a scene out of Hounds of the Baskerville", she whispered to herself. The vast forest held tall pine trees; the branches full and deep green in color. Small branches and stems lined the well beaten path and gathers of dried pine needles littered the forest floor. A few yards away, small animals timidly hid in the hollowed out logs that had years ago fallen and become a part of the forest floor. Bailey took a few hesitant steps closer to the deeper part of the forest and then stopped suddenly as she heard a slight rustle that was surely not the wind. Her heartbeat quickened and she felt a small bead of sweat leave the nape of her neck and travel down to the front of her chest.

"Hello?" she called softly. Bailey listened for a moment and then giggled nervously. "Only me", she said out loud. "It's not like the axe murderer or serial killer is going to answer me."

"Oh, I wouldn't be so sure of that", a deep voice said softly behind her.

Bailey's breath hitched suddenly. Every nerve in her body seemed to be on edge and she stood rigid; her feet not willing themselves to move.

"Scared?" he asked slowly. Bailey stayed perfectly still and silent.

"Don't be. I won't hurt you." He chuckled softly. "But I do have to wonder why a pretty",(he walked around her slowly) "young", (he reached out a let a few strands of her shoulder length, curly hair run through his fingers) "thing", he said, coming around to face her, "would be doing all alone in the dark, deep in the forest?"

Bailey willed her eyes to look up and she stared into the most handsome face she'd ever seen. Although it was still quite dark, she had no problem making out his strong, yet pleasant facial features. He had gorgeous hazel brown eyes and a strong jaw line. His nose was perfect, not too big, or too long and skinny. His lips were pouty and tinged a light pink. His skin was a color that she could only describe as coffee with a lot of cream in it. Just how she liked her coffee.

"Why?" she muttered under her breath. "Why is it that all the cute ones are always crazy?"

"Because the ugly ones are clinically insane", he said, leaning into her closely. "Us cute ones", he whispered as he got closer, "are crazy, yet functional." He laughed at his joke and leaned back against a nearby tree. "I'm Charles, and contrary to popular belief, I'm not crazy. I'm one of the owners of this property and as pretty as you are, you are trespassing."

Bailey stepped back and sized him up. Usually full of sass, Bailey's brain and quick tongue failed her.

"Nothing?" Charles said with a short laugh. "Nothing to say? Not even an 'I'm sorry Mr. Wentworth, it won't happen again, Mr. Wentworth, or...'"

"Wentworth?" Bailey said, cutting him off, and finding her voice. "Charles Wentworth the Second?"

"The Third, actually", he said. "The Second is my father. You know of my family?"

"I've only read about them", Bailey replied, her body easing into a more relaxed state.

"Are you into agriculture?" he asked. "Most of the people that come looking for us are either agriculturalists or wannabe..."

"Sort of", she said, cutting him off again. "My real passion is writing and doing research on, well, never mind." She reached for her rather large backpack to the right of her. "I *am* sorry, Mr. Wentworth", she said earnestly. "I'll get off your property now." She turned to leave and walk back when he reached out for her.

"Let me guess", he said, grabbing her backpack from her suddenly. "You're a ghost hunter?"

"No", she said, looking at him quite intently. "I'm interested in the paranormal and its effects on nature. "I don't do", she said using air quotes, "ghosts."

"My apologies", Charles said. "I didn't mean to offend you. I didn't know that there was a difference."

"There is", Bailey said. "And it's no problem. It's just... there is something about this place." She sighed heavily. "I have no idea why, but I feel something when I'm here. Like, someone is watching over me. Or like someone is trying to connect to me. I don't know, maybe I am crazy."

"Maybe you are", Charles said, smirking at the shocked look on her face. "But remember, the cute ones are the functional kind of crazy."

Bailey laughed and Charles thought he'd never heard a more pleasant or exciting sound.

"It's cold", Charles said, noticing Bailey shivering in her light jacket. "Why don't we go up to the main house and warm up for a minute?"

Bailey nodded and followed him up the pathway back to the edge of the property towards the structures. The lawn here was beautifully manicured and surrounded by well-planned, mature trees. As they walked, Bailey looked up and saw the prettiest Victorian manor she'd ever laid eyes on. The Painted Lady stood two stories high, with an east and west wing attached. There was a carriage house behind it, a greenhouse to the left and only what Bailey saw in her dreams, a large barn with stables to the right.

"You live here?" Bailey said in awe.

Charles smiled widely at her. "Yes I do. I'm in the west wing. My father and mother have the east wing and we share the main house."

They climbed the stairs together and when Charles held the door open for Bailey he donned a butler-like voice. "Welcome to Wentworth Manor", he sang out.

Chapter 2

Bailey giggled slightly and entered. Not more than 3 feet in, she stopped and gazed with open mouth. The foyer in which they stood had high vaulted ceilings, with turn of the century wainscoting and crown molding. The hard wood floors were original to the home which, if Bailey guessed, was built in the early 1900's.

"Beautiful", Bailey said. "Absolutely gorgeous."

Charles looked up and noticed what Bailey was staring at. He had lived his whole life in the manor and had always appreciated the eye that his forefathers had for style and flare.

"Yes it is." Charles agreed. "When the manor was renovated in the early 2000's, my mother had a lot of input as to preserving the home's original character. Modernizing it was out of the question. The home has modern appliances, of course, and state of the art sound and surveillance, which, by the way is how I found you", he said, nudging her softly. "The original character was kept the same, paying homage to the wonderful builders of early Victorians."

A sweet and slightly plump lady appeared in the hall and smiled brightly.

"Charlie!" she bellowed, walking as fast as she could and embracing him tightly when she reached him. Wearing a cream house robe with what

Bailey thought had to be real fur around the collar, this woman was the air of elegance and dignity. Bailey almost felt the need to curtsy.

"Hi Mama", Charles said, hugging her back. "You're walking better!"

"I'm doing water aerobics every morning! If your father had his way, I'd be in the pool all day long" she gushed. "Look! I lost 50 pounds in total!"

"You'll waste away to nothing you keep that up!" Charles said, laughing. His mother, although not obese, was not what anyone would call skinny. She was, as her husband would say, pleasantly plump. But ever since the doctor became concerned with the fluid retention on her legs and feet, the family had taken a more active role in her health. No way was the Wentworth family going to lose their beloved matriarch anytime soon.

"I wasn't expecting to see you until tomorrow", she said, oozing southern charm and an even thicker accent. "I thought you'd be holed up in your wing for another day." She looked to her left. "And who is this beautiful creature?" she said, walking over to Bailey and wrapping her in a humongous hug.

"I, um, don't rightly know, Mama", Charles said.

Without missing a beat, Bailey responded with her name, her voice muffled by the fact that her face was being stuffed in the woman's large bosom. "Bailey Matthews", she added.

"What a lovely name, Dear", Mrs. Wentworth said, releasing Bailey from her embrace. "And Charlie, don't say 'um'. It's undignified."

"Yes Ma'am", he said, with a smile.

She turned back to Bailey. "I'm Jane Wentworth. But everyone calls me Janey. Charles Alexander Wentworth the Third, how could you bring a girl home and not know her name?"

"Well, we just met, Ma'am", he said with a grin. "I brought her here because I found her trespassing in the forest", he said, winking at Bailey.

"Oh Charlie, you didn't call the authorities, did you?" Janey said, her hands firmly on her hips.

"No Ma'am", Charles said. "I brought her up to warm up a bit. I thought", he said, siding up to his mother and kissing her cheek, "some of your special cocoa could do the trick?"

"Oh you charmer, you", Janey said, blushing. "I'd be delighted!" She grabbed Bailey's hand. "Come with me dear! My cocoa is to die for!"

Charles watched his mother and the very pretty Bailey walk semi-swiftly around the corner to the kitchen. He followed behind them a ways when he felt a firm but gentle hand on his shoulder.

"Son!" Mr. Wentworth bellowed.

"Dad!" Charles almost screamed as his father embraced him in a hug rivaling his mother's. "I thought you'd still be in Georgia!"

"I got back yesterday! I had to hurry home to your mother. Have you seen her? She's looking, well pretty um..."

"Dad!" Charles said chuckling. "TMI, Dad. And don't say 'um'. It is most undignified." he chuckled.

"You sound just like your mother." the elder Charles said, hugging his son tighter.

"It's good to be home. I missed you and Mom so much", Charles said.

"I missed you too, Son. I had no one to watch football with. Your mother is no fun with that. So, how was Europe? Tell me everything."

Charles stepped out of his embraced and smiled. His father was often called a "skinny Santa". He wasn't really skinny, but he wasn't portly either. His eyes were the deepest green, like sparkling emeralds. Whereas his mother's complexion was a deeper caramel from her African-American roots, his father's Irish background made his skin almost alabaster. What was once flaming red; his full head of hair and beard were now white as snow.

"Europe was amazing, Dad. I loved Spain, especially Madrid. I could have stayed in Ireland for a lifetime. But Paris, Dad. Paris captivated me. I could live there, for sure."

"I'm not surprised. Your mother and I spent a great deal of time in Paris in our younger years." He smiled brightly. "For a while, I thought for sure your mother was going to camp out and live at the base of the Eiffel Tower."

Chapter 3

"Live where, Dear?" Janey said, coming around the corner, carrying a tray of steaming hot cocoa and Bailey walked beside her, carrying a plate of cookies that she was eyeing very hungrily.

"Oh, Janey! Cookies and cocoa! You're too much, Doll", Charles the Second said with a grin. "And I said that you practically lived at the Eiffel Tower when we were in Paris."

"Oh I really did", Janey said, passing out cups of cocoa to everyone. "I felt a kind of calm there. It was like I was supposed to be there. I felt as if someone or something was calling me there."

Bailey looked at Janey intently. Hadn't she just said the same thing about the forest?

Charles the Second took a sip and looked up. "And who is this pretty young thing?" he said, reaching for Bailey's hand and kissing it softly.

Bailey giggled, looking at the older man. 'Like father, like son', she thought.

"Bailey, Sir", Charles said. He winked at his dad. "I found her trespassing on the grounds."

"Then by all means, no cookies and cocoa for her then", he said, trying to be serious. The twinkle in his eyes gave him away. "Oh, who am I kidding? Feed that child!" he said, giving her two more cookies. Where Janey was the disciplinary in the family, Charles the Second was a gentle teddy bear. He had a soft spot for his children and grandchildren and Janey often scolded him for spoiling them rotten, although she often did the same thing behind his back.

"I honestly didn't know I was", Bailey said of her trespassing. "I've been coming to the forest for a few months now. I can't really explain it; something draws me there. I get to the glen next to the forest and this euphoric feeling overwhelms me. I have literally sat in the forest for hours, just meditating and listening to the sounds." Bailey took a bite of her cookie and sighed happily. "These are so good, Mrs. Wentworth."

"Thank you, Dear", she said. "And it's Janey." She took a sip of her cocoa and looked intently at Bailey. She reminded her so much of herself. So lost and unsure of herself, yet adventurous and courageous at the same time. It was time to dive deeper. "Don't your parents worry?"

Bailey sat quiet for a moment. A solemn look washed over her face and Janey understood it immediately. Before Bailey could reply, Janey sat her cup down and folded her hands. Charles the Second and Charles looked at each other and smiled.

"Will you excuse us?" Janey said, looking at Bailey but speaking to the men in the room. On cue, the men got up, grabbing cups and cookies and headed for the kitchen. Charles looked over at Bailey and winked. He mouthed, "It's OK" and gave her a thumb's up as he closed the door behind him.

Janey looked at Bailey, took her hand and patted it. "Are you orphaned, Dear?"

"You don't bite your tongue, do you?" Bailey said with a chuckle.

"No I don't. I know a roamer, as I like to call them, when I see one. I used to be one, well until my husband's parents found me. You know, you remind me of me at your age. I'm guessing, 24?"

Bailey looked shocked. "You'd be right. That's amazing!"

"You brave girl", Janey said. "I know all too well that struggle. May I ask how it came to be?"

Bailey grabbed her cup again. "I lost my mother when I was 15. My father was in the military and after she died, I followed him from base to base. After an honorable discharge, he moved us to New York and went to work for the NYPD. My father passed away after 9-11. He was a first responder and then died shortly after saving several people."

"What a tragedy", Janey said, patting her hand. "How did you come to Virginia?"

"I stayed in New York for a few years after, went to NYC, but the pain was just too much to bear. All the rest of my family is scattered abroad." She sighed. "The joys of being an army brat."

"I'm sorry, I don't know those woes", Janey said. "I was a child of the 60's. I was dragged to sit-ins and rallies. My mother was pregnant with me soon after she met my father. He's an ex-Black Panther."

"I read a lot of the struggles of our people", Bailey said. "Or rather half my people. My father was Eastern European, and my mom was African-American."

"It was a difficult time, for sure", Janey said. "My mother was determined to let me have another life. When I was 11, I was sent to a boarding school here in Virginia. I loved it here so much, I stayed."

"Did you have to encounter a lot of racism when you went to school?" Bailey asked, grabbing another cookie.

"You have a great appetite", Janey said of her hunger for knowledge and cookies. Bailey smiled goofily and bit her cookie again. "And yes, I encountered some. But let me teach you something very quickly. Racism and prejudice are two different things. Racism is the belief and acting on the notion that your race, your whole entire race is better than another. Prejudice is the belief and acting on the notion that you yourself are better than anyone else, regardless of race, creed, color, religion, etc. I've seen some racism. I've *experienced* a lot of prejudice."

Bailey sat in front of the woman looking utterly dumbfounded.

"I'm assuming no one ever taught you the difference?" Janey said, drinking deeply from her favorite mug.

"No Ma'am", Bailey said.

"It's imperative that you recognize the difference between the two", Janey said. "They both still exist, and have been cloaked with a deep cover of invisibility. You may not see them until they are right there in front of you. And even then, it may be difficult to detect."

"Wow", Bailey said, marveling at the woman.

Chapter 4

Janey and Bailey sat in the lounge for some time, eating cookies and drinking cocoa. The room was very warmly decorated; accents of browns, tans and creams everywhere. To the right was a lit fireplace, bringing a stream of heat into combat the chilly weather the late winter night had to offer.

The men sat in the library across the hall trying not to laugh.

"She's getting read, isn't she?" Charles asked his father.

"Probably. You know your mother hasn't really been the same since Mary left." Charles the Second said.

"She misses having Sis around, I know", Charles said.

"It's not just that, although it does play a tremendous part. It's having another woman to talk to, someone to have tea with and shop with. Mary stays busy between the boys and her work." He looked at his son and winked. "Be prepared, Son. She may just keep Bailey." His father studied him closely. "And if I'm not mistaken, you wouldn't have it any other way."

Charles looked at his father and tried to hide the truth that was painted across his face. "OK, you got me." He sighed.

"How long have you known she was on the grounds?" his father asked.

"I guess in all, about a week altogether. I saw her a few days before I left. When I returned a few days ago, I saw her again. Dad, she intrigues me. I mean, we get our share of wacko's looking for the 'haunted' forest, but she's a bit different. She wants to know what the earth knows."

"If you start singing 'Colors of the Wind', I'm leaving", Charles the Second said.

The men continued their talk until they heard an audible gasp from Bailey.

"Ah", Charles the second said. "We must be at the bargaining part." He said, hearing his wife talking.

As they continued their talk, Bailey became more and more intrigued with the older woman. She imagined that this is what it would have been like if her mother had lived. Having heart to heart talks over cocoa and cookies and such. Bailey smiled deeply as she sat mesmerized by Janey. Could you fall in love with a mother figure?

"The school I went to made me a southern lady", Janey continued. "The School of Hard Knocks taught me to use my position as a lady to make it in this world." She paused and looked at Bailey with deep interest. "You search the paranormal, don't you?"

"Yes", Bailey said.

"You question the earth. I can sense that. You know, I think I'd like to take you under my wing, if you'd like." Janey smiled at her for the first time during the conversation and Bailey instantly relaxed, not feeling so much like she was in an interview.

"I appreciate it, but how could I even afford..." Bailey started.

"Tut, tut", Janey said, interrupting. "You have something of great value to me; knowledge. As my husband said, I spent a lot of time at the Eiffel Tower in Paris. I believe you can help me there."

"Really?" Bailey said bewildered.

"Absolutely. Now, I know you and my son have just met..." Bailey blushed deeply as Janey continued. "But I can see the way you steal glances at each other. There is an obvious attraction there, and that's step one. Step two, well, as much as I've taken a liking to you, Dear, you need to be, well..."

"Groomed?" Bailey said, biting back a small chuckle.

"Oh, Dear, I hope I haven't offended. You're perfectly wonderful, and I don't want you to lose your essence, but there will be some things you would need to know if you want to get further in this world. Even I recognized that. Am I correct in assuming that you have a degree?"

"Two in fact", Bailey said. "A Bachelor's of Science in English and a Master's in English with a Specialization in Writing."

"I'm impressed", Janey said. "So, is it a deal?" She stood up and offered the young woman her hand.

"I'm a bit confused", Bailey said, accepting her hand. "What all is this entailing?"

"Answer me this, where do you live?" Janey asked.

"Um..." Bailey said.

"Don't say 'um' Dear. It's so undignified." Janey replied.

"Yes Ma'am." Bailey smiled. "I'll say that I'm between housing at the moment."

"Well then. As you say, this will *entail* you taking the room in the upper main house. You will stay here with us, and I'll impart on you all of my knowledge. I'll teach the ways of the Southern Lady, and pretty soon you'll be coming out at your own cotillion." At this, Janey practically gushed. "I do love a cotillion!"

"And, what, may I ask, can I offer you in return?" Bailey said through a smile, as she bit back a little laugh, seeing the older woman so emphatically giddy over just the thought of a party.

"You're going with me to Paris", Janey said matter-of-factly. "We're going to find the reason why I am drawn there. But there will be time for that later. It's very late, and a lady is hardly up past midnight, if she can help it."

"Then I suppose we can't help it, because it is after one am", Bailey said, with a small giggle. "I honestly don't know what to say to your generosity."

"Think nothing of it. And first lesson", Janey said, taking her hand as she stood. "Never admit to being at a loss for words. I find it best that when you can't find the words, a smile and nod will suffice. This gives you time to find the words, or, if you're in the presence of someone being quite foolish, give them time to hang themselves with their own words." Janey laughed a bit and smiled. "I've been in that position numerous times. You'll find, my dear, the people who are the least educated, loud, brash and foolish, often talk quite a bit. And they speak mostly nonsense." Janey yawned and led Bailey out the lounge.

Chapter 5

The men were waiting in the hallway as they exited.

"My Dear, you look positively beat", Charles the Second said, grabbing his wife's hand. "Let me get you to bed", he said wiggling his eyebrows at her.

"Oh you!" Janey said, playfully patting his arm and letting him lead her to the East wing. "Charlie, be good enough to show Bailey to the main room P, please", his mother said. "I do believe it's her favorite color."

"Ah", Charles said, picking up her backpack and hoisting it onto his back. "So, my mother has invited you to stay."

"Yes", Bailey said. "In exchange for... you know I'm not exactly sure what she expects of me."

"My mother is very sweet, kind, and loving. For sure, in my mother's mind, there is an even exchange. So for the room, board and whatever else she offers, believe me, whatever she asks of you, she sees as an even exchange. She will never hold it over you, and you won't owe her anything." He led her up two flights of stairs and opened the door on the left. When Bailey walked into the room, her eyes bulged out and her mouth dropped to the floor.

"Oh my word!" Bailey said.

"She's rubbing off on you already", Charles said, chuckling softly, gazing at Bailey who was looking around the room in amazement. The four-post queen sized bed was beautifully decorated with a lavender and white chenille bedspread and lots of fluffy white and dark purple pillows. The window curtains were sheer white with lavender and green flowers and dark oak hardwoods planked the floor. There was a dark oak vanity and matching dresser on the opposite wall. Two matching night stands donned each side of the bed and a chaise lounge stood in front of the window; the cushions a deep, velvet purple.

"It's absolutely stunning", Bailey said.

"Very", Charles said, looking only at her.

"How did she know that I loved purple?" Bailey asked.

"My mother is very good at reading people. In just a few minutes, she can guess most of the things people try to hide. It unhinges some people. Others..." he said looking at Bailey, "merely just become amazed by her."

"She is definitely amazing." Bailey sat down in the chair near the bed. "Where does that door lead?" she asked, pointing to the left.

"That would be your bathroom and closet", Charles answered.

"No way!" Bailey said.

Charles laughed and followed her into the large ensuite. There was a large shower, with a ledge seat and beautifully tiled with subway style tile. Two rain shower heads adorned the top and body heads were along the side of the walls. A large soaker tub was to the right a ways and a barn door on a slider hid the large walk in closet. Bailey stepped in and looked through the clothes that hung in there. They were mostly her size.

"Was she expecting me?" Bailey said aloud.

"Maybe", Charles said with a grin.

"How long have you known that I'd been coming to the forest?" Bailey said, facing Charles.

"Honestly?" he replied.

"Yes, please", Bailey said, crossing her arms.

"About a week in total", he said with a slight grin.

"And your mother?"

"Just met you today, although I did mention to her you were about Mary's size." Charles looked through the closet. "Hmm. She did a nice job."

"Who's Mary?" Bailey said quizzically.

"My sister. She married my brother-in-law Robert Cart..."

"Cartwright?" Bailey said. "Your sister is fashion expect Mary C. Cartwright?"

"Yes", Charles said. "I hate that she's so far away in New York. I miss her and my nephews."

"She has an amazing eye for design", Bailey said. She went back inside the closet and pulled out a dress. She looked at the tag and gasped. "Ralph Lauren?"

"Probably", Charles said.

She rifled through some more. "Donna Karen. Christian Dior. Good grief." Bailey walked out the closet and sat down again. "Those clothes cost just as much as my education."

"I didn't peg you as one into designers", Charles said.

"I'm not really. I like awards shows", she said, walking back over to the chaise lounge and sitting down. "Watch enough of them, and you learn designers. My dad and I used to watch them and then rag on the bad ones." Bailey laughed. "Oh, wait. Does that make me a bad person?"

Charles sat down next to her and smiled. "No. Not at all. It does make you adorable." He looked at her intently for a moment. Before Bailey knew what was happening, his soft lips were brushing against hers. A tingle with the power of lightning went coursing through her veins and Charles deepened the kiss, letting his hands tangle themselves in her soft hair. A muffled moan came from the pit of her stomach and Charles broke the kiss abruptly.

"Is something wrong?" Bailey said, as she sighed.

"I'm a gentleman. A Southern Gentleman. It's after midnight. I'm alone in a lady's room. If my mother saw me, she'd die." He smiled at her, and cupped her chin. "Not that I don't want to continue, but it wouldn't be right for me to stay any longer." He straightened up a bit. "There should be gowns in the bureau and feel free to shower if you feel the need. I doubt you'll start any training", he said, throwing air quotes around the word training, "tomorrow, so feel free to sleep in or at least until you smell pancakes."

Charles got up, took her hand and kissed it. "Until tomorrow, Bailey Matthews."

Charles smiled at her as he closed her door. Bailey sat there for a while, listening to the wind rustle outside the window. In just a few hours, she went from dreading heading back to the town over to find a place to sleep to being in a cushy, warm room with the Wentworth family. Anybody else would be wary; accepting an offer to be "groomed" and a place to stay. As Bailey stared out the window, she felt an excited rush of energy run through her. She had no idea what was about to happen, but she was anticipating it with an open spirit.

A tingle of a pulse resonated on her lips. Bailey lifted her fingers to her lips and smiled. The kiss from Charles was so unexpected. It had been so long since she had been kissed, she almost didn't recognize it. She got up and grabbed a gown from the drawer. Letting the beautiful, silky material flow over arms and hands, she twirled it around. After her shower, she snuggled down in the warm bed, replaying the last words Charles spoke to her as he left her room. "Wait", she thought to herself. "Pancakes?"

Chapter 6

Bailey awoke to the smell of pancakes in the air and the sound of sizzling bacon. For a moment, she was confused as to where she actually was. "The shelter on 5 th never serves bacon", she said aloud. She sat up and a flood of memories came rushing back at her: the chill of the night in the forest, the beautiful house, the intriguing conversation with Mrs. Wentworth, the amazing cocoa, and the kiss.

The kiss. She could still feel the slight tingle of lighting coursing through her. On her lips she could still feel sensation of his lips imprinted on hers. She showered quickly and chose a cute white capris pant with a lavender polo top from the closet. She threw her curly brown hair in a loose ponytail and headed down the stairs to the kitchen. Bailey took her time on the plush carpeted stairs, admiring the woodwork of the railing and banisters. The familiarity of this house was starting to haunt her and she made a mental note to try to remember where she'd seen this architecture before.

"Good morning", Bailey called out to no one in particular. She peeked around the corner on the first floor in the kitchen. Empty. She went to the lounge she sat in last night with Janey and the men and found no one. Bailey felt stymied. These were the only two rooms she had visited in the house. 'Well', she thought. 'I guess it's time to explore.'

Bailey went down the hall a bit and found a bathroom, a library, (she made a mental note to visit this room again) a billiard room, and a large room with a piano, a bar and seating.

"Wait a minute", Bailey said out loud. "Library, billiard room, lounge, conservatory, bathroom, kitchen, all the rooms of..."

"Clue", Charles said, coming up behind her softly.

Bailey jumped slightly and playfully punched his arm. "How do you do that?"

"I was taught at an early age to walk softly and carry a big a stick. A man should tread softly, but with swiftness and force."

"You do it well", Bailey said. "So this house is modeled after Clue?"

"My mother's favorite movie", Charles said.

"Mine too!" Bailey said excitedly. "I was wandering around looking for someone. I didn't see anyone in the kitchen."

"That's because we're in the dining room", Charles said, leading her down the hall and around the kitchen. "We very seldom eat in there unless it's a late night snack. And really, not very late because Mama says that a lady..."

"...hardly stays up after midnight, unless she can help it", Bailey finished. "I'm learning."

"Yes you are", Charles said, as he leaned down slightly and kissed her cheek. He looked deep in her eyes and mimicking the night before, kissed her deeply with passion and urgency. That familiar tingle surged through Bailey again, and they only parted the kiss when a 'tut, tut' was heard.

"The lady", Charles the Second said, "has not had breakfast yet. You can devour her afterwards." He laughed heartily. "I was sent to find you two. Breakfast is getting cold."

"I found her, and I was bringing her to breakfast", Charles said sheepishly.

"As you kids say, 'yeah, OK'", Charles the Second said, chuckling as he sauntered off around the corner.

Bailey blushed slightly and followed Charles around the corner to the dining room. And again, Bailey's eyes bulged. On the large, rectangular table were platters and platters of food. Bacon, eggs, sausages in links and patties, hash browns, pancakes, croissants, rolls and of course biscuits with sausage gravy.

Mrs. Wentworth looked up and smiled. "I thought you had gotten lost, Dear", she said, smiling at Bailey. "I sent my son to find you, but I assume he only aided you in getting further into your state of being lost." She laughed softly. "How did you sleep?"

"Very well", Bailey replied. "Thank you very much."

"You are most welcome", Janey said, smiling. "You're not going to need much under my tutelage, are you?"

"I can, and will learn a lot from you, Janey", Bailey said. "Besides, I will never deny you a chance at a cotillion."

At the mention of cotillion, Janey lit up like a Christmas tree. "Oh yes! Thank you for reminding me. I need to get the ball rolling. Literally."

Bailey sat down next to Charles and after grace was said, began to dig in when platter after platter of food was passed her way.

"You have a good appetite", Charles whispered to her.

Bailey took a sip of her coffee. "My father used to say I ate like a horse. A thoroughbred." Bailey smiled. "I eat, but I try to stay active."

"It shows", he whispered in her ear and Bailey blushed a deep crimson.

The foursome ate lazily, conversation flowing like honey on pancakes, which coincidentally, is how Mrs. Wentworth takes her pancakes.

Chapter 7

"How about we take a ride?" Charles said. He and Bailey were lounging on the lanai on his side of the house.

"In a car?" Bailey said, as she sipped her iced water.

"No..." Charles said, smiling at her. "I saw you eyeing the stables when we walked up to the main house last night. Do you ride?"

"I...don't", Bailey said, fighting the urge to say 'um'. "I love horses; I think they are beautiful creatures. But I have never ridden one in my life."

"Well that, my beautiful Bailey, is about to change", Charles said. "Has your food settled?"

"I think so", she said. She jumped up and down for a few times. "I feel OK", she said.

Charles groaned inwardly as he watched Bailey jump up and down in front of him. He turned away from her for a moment to take a few deep breaths. At this rate, he'd be repeating the cold shower from last night after the searing kiss they shared.

It had been innocent at first. He had wanted to see if her lips were as soft as they looked. He had known about her visiting the grounds for about a week. He watched her meditate and leave the forest at all hours. He had to admit, she intrigued him. He watched her carry a backpack big enough to put a body in. One night, when she dragged it out the forest, he thought that there just might be.

The more he watched her, the more he needed to know who she was. When he leaned in last night for a sweet good-night kiss, he was not expecting electricity to surge through his body. It caught him off guard, so much so that he had to end the kiss. If he hadn't, well, he might have found himself being most ungentlemanly.

"Earth to Charles", Bailey said with a small laugh.

"I'm sorry", he said, facing her. "You were saying?"

"I was saying that I feel perfectly fine to learn how to ride today." She had her hand on one hip and her other shading her eyes as she gazed at him.

Charles thought for a moment about her bouncing and quickly thought of another idea. "I was thinking of doing the practical stuff first before we hop on the horses. Maybe we can explore your first idea."

Bailey didn't try to hide her disappointment.

"Oh, don't look so sad", Charles said. "I'll even let you pick which car we take."

"Which car?" Bailey said incredulously.

"Yeah", Charles said. "Grandfather loved his cars. "When he passed away, he willed them my dad. Dad can't stand them, so I have free reign." Charles led her to a large enclosed car port. Inside there was a vintage Rolls Royce, a Mercedes, two Crown Victoria's, a Chrysler Spyder Eclipse convertible, and Sebring convertible.

"The Sebring", Bailey said without hesitation.

"The lady knows what she likes", he said, leading her to the mint green, pristine conditioned car. "Why this one?"

"Did you ever see the movie Waiting to Exhale?" Bailey said.

"I may have", Charles said.

"There is this one scene where one of the main characters, Savannah, is driving on the desert highway with a scarf around her head, blowing in the wind and listening to this really pretty, relaxing song. I always envisioned myself doing the same. And I fell in love with the car as soon as I saw it." Bailey ran her hands along the side of the car and sighed. "One day."

"How about today?" Charles said, tossing her the keys and catching her off guard.

"Say what?" Bailey said, recovering the keys from a fumble.

"You can drive, right?" Charles said, stopping at the passenger side.

"Yeppers skeppers!" Bailey said and Charles choked on a laugh.

"Yeppers skeppers?" Charles said, and then doubled over in laughter. "Adding to your beauty, and the whole paranormal thing, now you're goofy?"

"You seem surprised", Bailey said. "I also answer the phone 'ahoy'. I find it utterly redundant to say hello or hi twice."

Charles laughed even harder at her last statement and pulled her into a hug. He was mesmerized at how well they fit together. His head rested comfortably on the top of hers and his arms wrapped around her full but soft frame.

Charles the Second and Janey were strolling on the grounds when he saw the open carport door.

"I guess the kids decided to go for a drive after all", he said, holding his wife's hand as they walked along. They peeked inside for a moment and smiled watching the two embrace momentarily. As the kids let go of the embrace and got in the car, with Bailey at the helm, Mrs. Wentworth sighed.

"Remember when we used to go for rides like that?" she said.

"May I take you for a ride, Janey Dear?" Charles the Second said, steering her towards the port as the kids sped off.

"Not at the moment", Janey said. She unhooked her arm from her husband and surprised him by briskly walking away, winking an eye at him as she did.

"Oh you vixen, you!" he said, catching up with her and leading her to their side of the house.

Chapter8

Bailey and Charles drove through the countryside, listening to music, singing along horribly with the radio and laughing nonstop.

"I cannot remember the last time I had this much fun!" Charles said, as he watched Bailey guide the car over next to a small patch of woods.

"This was fun", she said, agreeing. "The last time I had this much fun, well, it was with my dad." Bailey said, cutting the engine off and leaning back in the seat. "He would always take me on these, 'let's get lost and find our way back' adventures." She smiled to herself. "Sometimes we'd be 'lost' for hours."

"Wait a minute. Wasn't your father a police officer? Don't they have to know their way around the city?" Charles asked.

"Precisely. I didn't even realize what he was doing. He knew where we were going. It was to instill survivalist skills in me. It was for me to have fun." She stopped talking and sighed. "After mom died, it was always about me. Maybe that's what makes me so interested in the unknown. I think…"

"Yeah?" Charles said.

"I think I'd like to talk to him one more time. To say thank you, at least. I want to thank my dad for being a great dad and an even greater man."

"Search all you want", Charles said, taking her hand and pulling her close. "But I guarantee he already knows how you feel."

As much as Bailey didn't want to, she couldn't stop herself. There in Charles' arms, safe and protected, she cried. Huge tears fell down her face, and her body shook momentarily as she sobbed for her life, the loss of her parents, and the hardships she endured. She never even realized how much she needed to be rescued until she met Charles. Bailey had always been her own Prince Charming. Well, at least until she met a real one.

When her tears subsided and Charles handed her his handkerchief to dry her eyes, Bailey smiled at him.

"I don't cry. I mean, I never cry. I didn't cry at my mom's funeral, and I didn't cry at my dad's." She wiped her eyes. "I'm sorry."

"Don't be", he said, kissing her forehead softly. "Everyone needs that release sometimes." Charles sat tall in his seat and mimicked who Bailey guessed to be his grandfather, because his father didn't seem the type to say those words.

"Wentworth men do not cry", Charles mimicked. "Tears are a sign of weakness and Wentworth men are not weak." Charles said, and then proceeded to laugh hysterically. "I hardly ever saw my grandfather smile. And when he did, it was usually at my grandmother. When she died, his smile went away permanently. After that, Dad made sure that Mary and I knew that crying was allowed, smiling was encouraged and hugs were the norm. He didn't want his children to grow up cold and distant." He hugged Bailey close to him and smiled. "Cry all you want."

Bailey chuckled softly. "I think I'm OK, thanks." She sat up straight in her seat and readjusted her mirror. "Where to now?" she asked.

Charles took a moment and looked around at where they were. A small wooded area was to their left and to the right a large open pasture. They were very close to home. There was a mist rising from the wooded area, several inches above the low lying mist that was already there. If Charles didn't know better, he could have sworn it was taking the shape of a ...

"Um Bailey?" Charles said.

"Charles, don't say 'um', it totally undignified." Bailey said, and giggled.

"Bailey!" Charles said a little louder. He pointed in the direction of the human-like figure the mist was taking shape into and watched as her eyes finally left his face and looked upon what he was seeing.

Bailey couldn't explain it, but it was like she was being called. She got out of the car, and started to walk toward the mist. When Charles registered what was happening, he got out of the car and followed her. The closer he walked toward Bailey, the thicker the surrounding mist got. Charles couldn't see even mere inches in front of him and when he tried to say Bailey's name, his voice sounded muffled and low.

Bailey walked closer to the man-shaped mist and a smile spread wide across her face.

"Dad?" she whispered. Bailey took a step back and the misty figure took on a more feminine look.

"Mom?" Bailey said. A touch, much like a mother's caress grazed across Bailey's cheek and lingered there for a moment.

"Mom!" Bailey called again softly. "I've missed you so much."

Charles was moving with tentative steps towards Bailey. He could hear her muffled voice, and when he reached out for her in the mist, she found and grabbed his hand.

"You are where you belong", a soft voice echoed in the mist. As quickly as it rose, the mist died away, and left Bailey clutching at the mist with one hand and holding on to Charles' hand for dear life with the other.

"I love you", Bailey said, as the mist burned off in the glowing mid-afternoon sun.

Charles wrapped Bailey in a hug and held her close. "OK", he said with a chuckle in his throat. "Now I'm a believer. What just happened?"

"My mom", Bailey said. "How close are we to the house?"

"It's on the other side of the glen", Charles said, releasing her from his embrace and leading her back to the car.

"Don't think I'm crazy..." Bailey started.

Charles looked down in Bailey's eyes. "After what just happened? Crazy doesn't even cross my mind."

"I think she's whom I've been coming out here to see. She's been the one calling to me. And...she spoke to me" Bailey said.

Charles looked at her intently. "What did she say?"

"You are where you belong", Bailey said.

Charles looked down at the beautiful woman in his arms. He had no idea what was happening, it was a lot to process. Full of mystery and intrigue, this woman was beginning to become a part of his very being. And he liked it very much.

"Smart woman", he said, as he leaned down and kissed Bailey. As they kissed, again, lightning coursed through their bodies and the deeper they kissed, the stronger it became.

Bailey had never felt anything like this before. Charles hadn't either. And for two people who had never been electrified this way by a kiss, it could only the beginning of a new and adventurous life.

Chapter 9

Early summer was upon the small town in Virginia. Warmer weather prevailed and with the cotillion only a week away, Bailey had never seen the house so full of people. Usually, the only people she saw were Janey, Charles the Second, who she now referred affectionately to as Papa, and of course Charles. Since the woods incident, which was the buzz around the house after they returned, they had spent as many waking hours together as they could. Charles still had his responsibilities with his part of the corporation and his many charities, but every night belonged to Bailey. Most weekends as well.

Bailey studied hard under Janey's tutelage. Still a goofy spitfire, as Charles liked to refer to her, now she was more refined. When Mary came to visit, they shopped and bonded as well. She took an instant liking to Mary and Mary's boys already called her Aunt Bailey.

Her relationship with Charles blossomed quickly and deeply. If Bailey would admit it, she was head over heels in love with Charles. His family had quickly become her family and she couldn't envision being anywhere else.

On the evening of the cotillion, people started arriving, filling the conservatory. Many prominent members of the society were there, including the mayor.

"I'm so nervous", Bailey said, pacing back and forth in the lounge with Janey. "I think I might throw up."

Janey looked at her sternly.

"My apologies. Vomit. I feel as though I may vomit." Bailey said, and then leaned over on the desk nearby.

"Drink this", Janey said, handing her a small crystallized glass with clear liquid.

"What, may I ask, is this?" Bailey said as she took a sip. Instantly her stomach stopped being queasy and she felt better. "Are you magic, Janey?"

Janey laughed at her and took the drink from her hand. "No", she said, "but I've been to and in a few of these. I know those nerves all too well. Now turn around. Let me see you."

Bailey took a step back and turned slowly. The full length ecru dress was accented with a deep purple sash and her hair was pinned up in a soft bun with loose curls at the nape of her neck, accented with lavender and dark purple flowers. She wore matching gloves and her makeup was minimal. She opted for crystal slippers. She told Janey they made her feel Cinderella-esque.

"You look beautiful, Dear", Janey said, hugging her lightly.

"Thank you", Bailey said. "Do you think Charles with think so?"

Janey laughed slightly and hugged her again. "You could wear a garbage bag and he'd think you were gorgeous. Believe me when I tell you my son is crazy about you."

"Really?" Bailey said. She blushed deeply. "The feeling is more than mutual."

"Oh good!" Janey said. "I've been waiting on more grandchildren!"

Before Bailey had a chance to retort, the fanfare played, and her name was being announced.

"It's show time!" Janey said, practically pushing her out the door of the lounge.

Chapter 10

Bailey heard the fanfare and stepped out the lounge after a gentle shove from Janey.

"Thanks", she muttered under her breath as she approached the opening to the conservatory.

"Announcing, Ms. Bailey Marie Matthews", the announcer said, as she stepped up. The few friends she had made in town were there in similar dresses like Bailey's, but in matching pastels colors. The young ladies did a small spin and curtsied in front of her. They then did a small dance and when they parted from her, Charles stood on the other side of the room, drinking her in.

Charles walked across the room quickly, eager to be Bailey's first dance at her coming out party when a hand landed hard on his arm and spun him around.

"Well, as I live and breathe", the young lady said, her voice dripping with a southern drawl.

"Charlotte", Charles said, not looking at her.

"Charlie! Honeysuckle vine!" Charlotte said, pulling him closer to her.

"What do you want, Charlotte?" Charles said, irritation heavy in his voice.

"Come now, where are your manners?" Charlotte said. "You're in the presence of a lady, at a ball, who is vying for your attention. There's no need for rudeness, Charles."

Charles looked down at Charlotte for the first time and sighed, defeated. She really did have a point. "My apologies, Ms. Charlotte. What can I do for you?"

"That's better", she said. "Dance with me, kind Sir."

"I am sorry", Charles said, "But my first dance belongs to Ms. Matthews."

"Her?" Charlotte said. "The stray? What could you possibly see in her Charlie? I mean, you can put her in a dress, but that doesn't make her classy and elegant."

"She", Charles seethed at Charlotte, "has more class and elegance in her pinky finger than..."

"We were so good together", Charlotte said interrupting. "Don't you miss that?" she said as she started to finger the lapel of his fitted shirt.

"Not at all, Ms. Charlotte." Charles pulled away from her slightly. "Now, if you'll excuse me." He had locked eyes with Bailey and when she smiled at him, his whole face lit up. Charlotte noticed this and when Charles turned back to her to release her death grip from his arm, she pulled him down and kissed him hard on the mouth, eliciting gasps from several onlookers, Janey, Charles the Second and most importantly, a look of shock and hurt from Bailey.

When Charles pulled away from her vice grip and her assault on his mouth, he was so mad he was ready to breathe fire. He looked up and locked eyes with his mother who nodded curtly.

"Ms. Charlotte", Charles said loudly enough to get the attention of those around him. "That was inappropriate behavior. I am spoken for, and although I thank you for your interest, I am not interested in pursuing a relationship with you." Charles looked up to see Bailey, and found her gone from the room.

As he pushed past Charlotte to find Bailey, he hissed to her in a low voice. "Gentleman or not, if you have ruined things between Bailey and myself, you will feel my full wrath. If you think our breakup was something, you haven't seen anything yet. That, Ms. Charlotte, is a promise." He strode away, leaving a very scared and shocked Charlotte in his wake. Two very tall gentlemen came to either side of Charlotte and led her to the corner where Janey was waiting.

"My Dear", Janey said, her voice dripping with disdain. "I have no idea what you hoped to accomplish this evening, but if you've hurt Bailey in anyway, you will not like me very much."

"News flash, Old Lady", Charlotte spat. "I already don't like you."

"And you wonder", Janey said with a chuckle, "why Charles didn't want to be with you. No amount of refinement, *Dear*, can change the essence of someone. Good evening."

Before Charlotte could retort, the men gently led her out to the main hall and called her service to leave. They made sure she left before returning to the ball.

Chapter 11

"What a spectacle!" Mrs. Jennings said, coming into the bathroom. When Bailey saw the kiss, she politely excused herself from her small entourage and headed to the bathroom down the hall.

"Yes, Ma'am", Bailey said, patting her hands on her bouncing legs over and over again on the chaise lounge in the corner.

"Oh my Dear", Mrs. Jennings said, sitting down next to her. She plopped down and instantly began to chuckle. "Now when I get ready to get up, you're going to have to help me", she laughed politely. She patted her knee. "As I was saying, my Dear, what you witnessed was a desperate attempt to grasp at something that has been long over and done."

"My apologies, but I don't understand", Bailey said.

"Ms. Matthews", Mrs. Jennings said. "About two years ago, there was a scandal around these parts that had tongues wagging for months!" she said. "The love affair of the century was over. Charlotte Kincade and Charles Wentworth the Third were over, caput, done for."

"May I ask why?" Bailey said, genuinely interested.

"I was hoping you would", Mrs. Jennings said. "Charlotte and Charles started off as most couples do. They were seen everywhere together, and the word marriage was floating around here and there. Although", she said, looking around to see if anyone was joining them, "let Janey tell it, she would have died before that tramp became a Wentworth."

Despite her current state of emotions, Bailey smiled. "Tramp you say?" Bailey countered.

"Well that *is* the reason they broke up. Charles came back from an overseas trip earlier than expected and when he called on Charlotte, he found her in the arms of another man. Amongst other things", Mrs. Jennings said.

"Poor Charles", Bailey said, feeling genuine sympathy. 'No one deserves that kind of pain', she thought.

"Indeed. The break up was very loud and public. Rumor has it that she followed him out of the house in nothing but her knickers!" Mrs. Jennings laughed.

"How embarrassing!" Bailey said.

"Dear," Mrs. Jennings started. "What you saw was her last attempt to win him back before he proposes to you. Think nothing of it."

"I'm sorry, did you say propose?" Bailey said with shock when the door opened.

"There you are", Janey said. "My Dear, are you alright?" she said, embracing Bailey in a hug. "Bertha? What are you doing in here?"

"Just comforting the young one, Janey", Mrs. Jennings said with a smile. She stood with a little help from Bailey and embraced Janey.

"What nonsense have you been feeding her?" she said to Mrs. Jennings, good naturedly ruffling her feathers.

"Oh, just this and that, and letting our dear Ms. Matthews know that what she witnessed was an old tiger at the end of the line."

"A bit crude, Bertha, but very fitting", Janey said.

"I don't understand", Bailey said.

"Dear", Janey started. "Tigers are the most fierce when they sense their end of their lives. They will fight until the end, usually quite forcefully."

"Oh", Bailey said. "Did she know about the supposed proposal?"

"Bertha! Bertha, what did you say?" Janey said, looking a bit miffed.

"I..." Bertha stuttered when the door opened.

"Protocol be damned, I need to talk to Bailey!" Charles said, entering the bathroom with his eyes covered, and his arm jutted out in front of him grasping at air.

"It's okay, Son", Janey said through laughter.

Charles opened his eyes to find his mother, Mrs. Jennings and Bailey standing in a semi-circle looking at him very bemused.

"Bailey, I..." Charles started.

"It's okay", Bailey said, reaching for his hand. "Let's get out of here and go talk. Okay?"

"Yes!" Charles said, grabbing her hand and leading her back to the conservatory to the balcony.

"I think I need to explain", Charles said when they reached the balcony.

"Mrs. Jennings already did", Bailey said. "Besides, I saw that *she* kissed you and not the other way around."

"Just what did our dear, lovely, Bertha tell you?" he said, with a raised eyebrow.

"Well, she told me you and Charlotte used to date and that she hurt you very badly. I'm so sorry about that", Bailey said hugging him.

"History", he said, pulling out of her grasp. "What I need to know is if we're okay", he said, looking at her intently.

"We're okay", Bailey said. "I think I was more embarrassed than hurt."

"I'm sorry you even had to witness that", Charles said, enveloping her into a hug again. "Because it's you, Bailey. It's you I love."

"Oh Charles!" Bailey said. "I love you too."

He leaned down and captured her lips and again electricity surged through them deeply. When he broke the kiss, he looked deeply into her eyes.

"I also need to ask you something", Charles said.

"So it wasn't a joke?" Bailey said quietly with her hands over her mouth as she watched Charles get down on one knee and pull a silver box from his jacket pocket.

The ballroom ceased all activity as all eyes and ears went to the balcony, where the doors were inconspicuously opened to gain better hearing and sight.

"No, not a joke", Charles said. "The last few months with you have been the best of my life. I don't believe you have to wait years to know when something is right and Bailey, we're right."

Tears stung the corners of Bailey's eyes as he continued.

"Bailey Marie Matthews, will you make me the happiest man in the world? Will you marry me?"

Bailey stood in front Charles and contemplated his question. In front of her knelt a man that made her feel loved and wanted. In a very short time, she went from being all alone to having a mom, dad, a sister, nephews and friends. Best of all, she had Charles.

"Yes", she whispered.

"Speak up Dear, we can't hear you!" Mrs. Jennings said loudly while Janey jabbed her in the side. "What?" Mrs. Jennings bellowed. "I'm old; I can't hear that well anymore!"

Bailey looked down at Charles and smiled. "Yes!" she screamed. She looked over in the Conservatory. "Was that loud enough for you, Ms. Bertha?"

"Just fine, Dear", Mrs. Jennings answered as the crowd chuckled politely.

"Yes?" Charles repeated, putting the two carat white and purple diamond engagement ring on her finger.

"Yes! A million times yes!" Bailey said, jumping in his arms as soon as he stood up. They shared a tender kiss as the band struck up a song.

"I do believe I still owe you a coming out dance", Charles said, taking her hand and pulling her close.

"Yes you do and all the rest of my dances for the rest of our lives", she said as he twirled her around the floor and kissed her again.

Chapter 12

If Bertha Jennings thought that Charles' and Charlotte's break up was enough to get the town talking, then the coming out of a one Ms. Bailey Marie Matthews broke that record easily. For weeks all anyone could talk about was the Wentworth Cotillion and the embarrassment of one Ms. Charlotte Kincade. Since that night, Charlotte couldn't be spotted anywhere. Rumors flew around that she had run off with one of the security guards from the night of the cotillion that had mysteriously never shown up for work the next day. Some say she moved away in pure embarrassment.

Everywhere Bailey went, she was stopped people who congratulated her on her engagement and expressed their delight that she won Charles over the town's resident harlot. People she'd never even met spoke to her like she was born and raised in the town. She had to give it to Janey. When she brings you out, you come out!

Bailey had always been a loner, so it was a bit of a new essence to suddenly have invitations to bridal showers, brunches and other get-togethers with her new friends. She quickly learned that a great deal of the people around town were just like her, down to earth and sweet, but formal when they needed to be.

Janey sat the happy couple down in the library and began discussing the wedding plans.

"So, I wanted to ask something of you two", Janey said, her actions so uncharacteristically like herself.

Both Charles and Bailey looked at each quizzically. "What is it, Mama?" Charles answered.

"Well, it's been about three weeks since you two got engaged and you may have noticed I haven't planned one little thing", she said with a smile.

"I have noticed", Bailey said. "To be frank, I've been a little worried. I thought you might not be feeling well or worse, that you really didn't want..."

"If your next words are about you being my daughter-in-law, then hush. You are already my child, so that is definitely not the case. Also, I feel as spry as a slinky!" she chuckled, "Okay, maybe not a slinky. More like a coiled telephone cord. Do they still have those?"

"Mama", Charles said, edging her on.

"Alright. I want to go to Paris, preferably before you get married." Janey turned to Bailey. "My dreams have come back. I need to discuss these with you and I want to end it or begin it, which ever, now."

"We haven't really set a date, have we?" Bailey said, turning to Charles.

"No, we haven't. Although, there is a pressing matter I want to discuss with you about your down time."

"You've noticed it too, have you?" Janey said.

"What are you two going on about?" Bailey said, smiling. She saw the twinkle in both of their eyes. She had made mention to Charles the Second about feeling a little bored.

"I think you should pursue some sort of career, Bails", Charles said.

"After Paris", Janey said.

Bailey looked at the both of them. "I'd love to, but I haven't the faintest idea what I truly want to do. When I was younger I fancied being a writer. Especially writing on the paranormal, but as of lately, I haven't even had the urges to go to the forest."

Charles mockingly through his hands up and buried his face in chest. "Mama, I've broken her!" Charles said, trying to hide his smile.

"I'm not broken", Bailey said, laughing. "I'm just happy."

"Well", said a voice off from the side of the library door. "That's going to either decrease, or increase, depending on how you look at it."

"Papa!" Bailey said and immediately embraced him in a hug. He had been gone on another business trip. How she had missed him! Their talks and walks on the grounds were beginning to be a regular thing and she looked forward to them very much.

"PYT", he said, eliciting a deep laugh from Bailey. It was his pet name for her, reminiscent of the very first time he'd met her.

"What have you done, Dear?" Janey said, as he hugged her and kissed her sweetly.

"Well. I went and put those two degrees of hers to work." Charles the Second turned to his soon to be daughter in law. "English writing, correct?"

"Yes Sir", Bailey answered. "Now, what have you done to me?" she said, teasing him.

"My son's Feed the Homeless foundation is in need." Charles the Second said.

"I thought Sophia was going to fill that spot?" Charles asked, cutting in.

"She was, and then the funniest thing happened", his father answered.

"What did you do?" Charles said with a raised eyebrow.

"Listen, I'll take responsibility for my actions, but this I had no hand or anything else in this one", Charles the Second said with a chuckle.

"Oh!" Bailey said.

"What, Dear?" Janey said.

"Sophia's pregnant, isn't she?" Bailey said. She grabbed her cell phone and sent a quick text. A month ago, Sophia was in her entourage for the cotillion and Bailey noticed that she didn't drink that night. She never said anything, but now she knew!

"So, we are still in need of a head proposal and grant writer", Charles said. He turned to Bailey and so had Janey and Charles the Second. With Bailey oblivious to their stares, she answered the confirmation text on her friend's good news.

"What?" Bailey said, looking up into three pair of eyes staring intently at her.

"Are you interested?" Charles said.

"In Sophia's position? I don't know. She said her boss was a tyrant", Bailey said, trying to hide a smile.

"Hey!" Charles said, playfully punching her arm. "I am not a tyrant. A little overbearing, maybe, but you'd wouldn't be answering to me anyway", Charles said. "At least not for this position", he said, wagging his eyebrows in her direction.

"No?" Bailey said.

Charles physically turned her to directly face his father. "Meet your new boss."

She stood up and hugged him again. "I accept", Bailey said, smiling.

"Good", Janey said. "Now maybe we can get back to the Paris trip discussion."

Chapter 13

Janey tossed and turned in her bed for what seemed like hours. After a few more minutes, she screamed so loud she awoke Charles the Second and even Bailey was up. Electing to stay in her room in the main house until after the wedding, she met Charles in the hallway as they made their way over the elder's wing.

"What's wrong with Mama?" Charles said, reaching his father with Bailey in tow, looking extremely worried.

"She's asking for you, Sweetheart", Charles the Second said, grabbing Bailey's hand. "I think her dreams are getting worse."

Bailey rushed into the room and was instantly frightened by what she saw. Janey was a pale as a ghost. Her hair was visibly wet as were her bed clothes.

"Janey?" Bailey said, entering the room softly.

"Come", Janey said, and patted the bed beside her. Bailey climbed in the bed beside and looked worriedly at the woman. She'd grown to love her very much and if something ever happened to her...

"Stop that", Janey said, watching the young woman carefully. "I'm not going anywhere. But my dreams are becoming much more intense and I think it's time I tell you about them. I have the oddest feeling that they involve you."

"But how can that be? We've only known each other a short time!" Bailey exclaimed.

"I know. It baffles me too. But I believe our pasts..." Janey paused for a moment. "Let me ask you a question. Who is Gertrude?"

"Gertrude?" Bailey thought for a moment. "Oh! My father had an Aunt Gertrude by marriage. His mother's brother's wife. Gertrude Fair..."

"Fairlane?" Janey said, interrupting and sitting up abruptly.

"Yes, Gertrude Fairlane. But how did you...?" Bailey said.

"She's been in my dreams", Janey said. "She's been talking to me. Tell me, how did she die?"

Bailey took her hand. "Can you tell me?"

"Unsolved as far as the family knows but I saw it. I know it sounds crazy, but I saw it. I saw it when I was in Paris and I saw it just a few moments ago. Your great Aunt was murdered, Dear." Janey tried to hide it, but a solitary tear slipped down her cheek.

"You sound like my father. He always believed that too." Bailey sat back on the bed. "Wait a minute. Great Aunt Gertrude disappeared and she left my Grandmother a letter saying she was going to visit Paris but a few weeks later the family got a postcard from Paris, Texas!" Bailey said. "How can that be?"

"I think, if we can get to Paris, we might just find out", Janey said. "Honey?" Janey called out.

"I'm already on it", Charles the Second said, coming back in the room with his son in tow.

"On what? What's happening?" Charles said.

"Charlie, we're going to Paris. Bailey is connected to us deeper than even I thought", Janey said, as she motioned him to join them on the bed.

"She's dreaming about my great aunt", Bailey said, as Charles got in the bed and sat behind Bailey. Bailey leaned her head back against his chest and listened to his heartbeat, as Charles the Second sat at his desk on his laptop looking up airfares and hotels. Before Bailey knew anything, she had slipped off into a quick sleep.

The forest was still and dark. Bailey followed the well beaten path she had made into the deeper part of the forest. The mist was about ankle high, and the moon was full, although the trees did good job of blocking the light. Bailey walked deeper into the forest until she heard a soft rustle behind her.

"Hello?" Bailey called out. She stood still for a moment and listened. The rustling grew louder and she heard heavy footsteps approaching.

"Who's there?" Bailey called again. The footsteps got louder and louder and then Bailey felt something cold reach out and touch her, sending a chill through her body, starting her to shiver.

"Here", Janey said. "Put this over her." Charles pulled the chenille blanket over his sleeping fiancé and held her closer to him.

Bailey stopped shivering instantly and turned to face the direction of the footsteps. An image of a man, donning a policeman's uniform and a larger, heavyset woman stood side by side, smiling at her.

"So this is Bailey", the woman said. "I'm sorry I didn't have the chance to meet her in life, Brian", she said. "She reminds me of me; so adventurous and full of life. Although, she's a bit skinny if you ask me."

The man to the side of her chuckled softly. "You think any woman that isn't at least a size 18 is skinny." He turned to Bailey. "Hi ya, Toots."

"Daddy?" Bailey said, her face contorted in confusion.

Charles looked down at Bailey's face. She was starting to squirm in his arms and her eyebrows were furrowed hard. He started to wake her when his mother stopped him.

"Let her finish this", Janey said.

Bailey smiled brightly at the orb of her father before her, just as handsome as ever. "So then you must be, Great Aunt Gertrude?" Bailey asked.

"Oh Brian, you were right. She's smart, and definitely has the gift." Gertrude said. She turned her attention back to Bailey. "You would be right, Doll."

"Can you tell me what Jane Wentworth has to do with this?" Bailey asked.

"Just cut right to it, huh?" Gertrude said. "I like her, Brian." She smiled brightly. "I like Jane. She's a real peach. She has your gift too, although in her older age, it's not as strong as it used to be. That's why, well, I'll let Brian tell you that part."

"Gift? Dad?" Bailey said.

"Ever have déjà vu, Toots?" Brian asked.

"All the time", Bailey said.

"That's usually the first sign", Brian continued. "Even when you were younger, you seemed to know things others didn't. You could feel things more deeply. Your mom used to call you her little..."

"Poltergeist", Bailey finished. "I thought it was because I liked the movie so much."

"That too." Brian paused and a saddened look appeared on his handsome face. "Toots, you were the only one who believed me when I said Gertrude was in trouble. When you were younger, you would dream about her and tell me she was by the big pointy thing. It took me a while to figure out what you meant. One night, when you were sleeping, I went to your room to check on you and I heard you singing. You were singing 'Aleut et a' in your sleep and I couldn't remember teaching you that song. I asked your mom and she confirmed that she never taught you the song either. So I put two and two together, but when I told your grandmother, she wrote Gertie off as being flighty. I knew she wasn't though." He looked over at his aunt and smiled. "It felt good to know someone believed me even if it was my 10 year old daughter."

"What can I do?" Bailey said.

"You have to go with Janey to Paris. The answers are there. If you two do this, you can save her." Gertrude looked at Bailey intently. "You must hurry, Doll."

"Her?" Bailey said. "Wait, who?"

Bailey watched her father and Gertrude start to vanish when she yelled. "Daddy!"

"Yeah Toots?" he said, his image becoming more opaque by the moment.

"Thank you for taking care of me", Bailey said, as a tear slipped down her cheek.

"My pleasure, Sweetheart. I will always love you and I'll always be with you." His image vanished and as Charles was wiped Bailey's tear off her cheek, Bailey awoke with a start.

Chapter 14

"I need some air", Bailey said, climbing out of the California king-sized bed and exiting the room. Charles looked to his mother and when she nodded, he followed Bailey out into the hallway and onto the front porch.

"Bails", Charles said, catching up with her. "Wait a minute!" He caught up to her and gently grabbed her arm. "Bailey, what's wrong?"

Bailey faced her fiancé and couldn't stop the tears from flowing down her face. "I don't know what's happening to me. "I'm scared." She started to cry a bit harder as Charles embraced her.

"Okay", he said, trying to calm her. "I get that. Look, before you entered my life, the only weird thing around here was mother's uncanny ability to read people. She never really elaborated on what", he swirled his hand around in a circle, "this is. But whatever it is, we'll figure it out, together."

"I don't want to figure it out", Bailey said, pushing away from him. "It's one thing to get vibes in a forest and yes, seeing the misty form of my mom was, shall we say, a bit concerning, but this? This is too much!"

"What's too much?" Charles said. "Bailey, I saw you were dreaming. What did you dream about?"

"My father and my great Aunt Gertrude. They were speaking to me. In the forest. They told me to go the Paris with your mom. They said we can save her."

"Her? Her who?" Charles asked. "My mom?"

"I have no idea", Bailey said. "I asked, but they just vanished. I..." Bailey's voice got caught in her throat. "This is a lot, Charles, a whole lot."

"I know", he said, hugging her closer. "If I were you, I'd be terrified, but honestly, don't you want to know? I mean, you and my mother share this connection. If there is a possibility you can save her..."

"Or someone", Bailey finished. "I have no idea who I'm supposed to be saving."

"Or someone", Charles said. "Then don't you think you owe it to yourself to find out?"

Bailey sat down in the wicker chair on the left side of the porch. Her head was reeling and her body was exhausted. She felt like she'd run a marathon and swam through the English Channel.

"Okay", Bailey said weakly. "I'll go. I don't know what's going to happen, but I'll go. I at least owe that to your mother."

"You don't owe me anything, Dear", Janey said, joining them on the porch. She sat down wearily in a chair next to Bailey. "You don't have to go."

Bailey looked at Charles and then at Janey. The older woman's face was full of concern and love for her and her wellbeing. She could see that Janey was exhausted too. If she didn't go to Paris, Bailey guessed that this would only get worse. She didn't want to know what worse looked like.

"I'm going", Bailey said firmly. "We need to see this through." Bailey took her hand. "We need to go over these dreams together. That's where we'll start. Now, where we'll end up..."

"You'll be fine", Charles the Second said, joining them. "Now, everybody go get packed. Out plane leaves in 3 hours."

With their bags packed and the group freshly showered and dressed, Janey and Bailey sat side by side on the porch in the mid-morning air discussing the dreams again.

"With an axe, you say?" Bailey asked again, writing down the details in a small notebook.

"An axe, and a very rusty one at that. She was taken from the base of the tower." Janey wrung her hands. "How is she connected to me again?"

"She wouldn't say. She just said that she liked you, that you were a peach." Bailey patted Janey's hand.

"Had she'd lived, she'd be about my age, right?" Janey said.

"I gather so", Bailey answered.

"Perhaps we met in the past", Janey said, trying to search her brain for the answer.

"Maybe it will become clearer when we get there", Bailey said and then looked up when she heard the door open and close.

"So what's the plan?" Charles said, as he grabbed his mother's hand and helped her up to stand. He reached for Bailey's hand and repeated the gesture.

"As soon as we get there, we're going straight to the tower", Janey said. "I want this over with."

"I couldn't agree more", Charles the Second said. He chuckled a bit when they all turned abruptly and met him with a glaze. "What?" he said. "I want to sleep. I haven't been sleeping well. It goes without saying that I want you two ladies to have some peace of mind."

The cab pulled up and the foursome hopped in.

"So it begins", Bailey said, as they car sped off into the growing sunlight.

Chapter 15

Bailey sat back in her seat as the plane flew over Paris, readying its' descent into the Charles de Gaulle Airport. She honestly couldn't think of a prettier sight than the Eiffel Tower at 20,000 feet in the blazing morning light. Or more like early afternoon light. The six hour difference was going to take a little getting used to.

After customs, the foursome exited the airport and Janey took Bailey's hand and stepped on to French soil. The surge of electricity that ran through the both of them at the same time was like being hit by a bolt of lightning. Bailey felt electricity every time she kissed Charles, but this surge was different. This was definitely an affirmation for Bailey. If she had any doubt that she was supposed to be here, she didn't anymore. As the feeling ran through the pair of women, they stopped dead in their tracks, causing a few people to stop and notice.

"What have we gotten ourselves into?" Janey said, squeezing Bailey's hand.

"I have no idea. I was going to ask you the same question", Bailey said. The men stopped when they realized they were walking alone.

"Janey?" Charles the Second said. "Honey?"

"Bails?" Charles said, echoing his concern.

"We're okay, right Janey?" Bailey said, willing her legs to move. She began moving her legs and looked to the side at Janey. Janey nodded.

"We're good", Janey said, making her legs move as well.

"I wouldn't go as far as to say that", Charles said, watching his mother and fiancée closely.

"Let's go get checked in and get this over with", Charles the Second said, his voice dripping deep with worry. "I don't like this hold, or this, whatever this is, has on you two."

After checking into Hotel Pullman Paris Tour Eiffel, the four sat down for a quick game plan.

"Okay, so what now?" Janey said.

"Well, that depends. How do you feel?" Bailey asked, searching the woman's face for tell-tale signs of weariness or fatigue.

"I feel fine. I want to go the tower." Janey turned to her husband. "Thank you, Honey. I have no idea how you've put up with me all these years."

"Easy", Charles the Second said, kissing her cheek. "I gamble." He chuckled at his joke. "You know I love you, more than myself. I'd do anything for you and you really are easy. Loving you has always been easy." He helped her stand up and grabbed her purse.

Charles looked on at his parents and then at his bride-to-be who was staring lovingly at the older couple. Since the moment he had started dating, he had searched for what his parents had. He'd seen them argue, and he'd seen them love. He'd watch them sacrifice and compromise. Now, as he felt Bailey grab his hand, he sighed inwardly and contently. He had found what he had always wanted. He kissed Bailey's cheek and she giggled.

"OK", Charles said. "Let's go find out what this is all about."

Charles hailed a shuttle bus and they hopped in and headed to the tower. As Bailey got on the bus, she locked eyes with the driver. He was younger, about Bailey's age. His hair was deep blonde and Bailey noticed a small cut on his left cheek.

"Problem Miss?" the driver said smiling at her; his English covered with a French accent. No sooner than the words left his mouth, Bailey felt an uneasy feeling wash over and nauseate her severely.

"Miss?" the driver repeated. Bailey stared at him as she took a seat next to Charles.

"I'm not even going to ask if you're okay", Charles said. "I know better. So I'll ask, what just happened?"

"I'm not sure", Bailey said. "I just got this funny feeling and a wave of nausea hit me."

"Hmm. Maybe we should have eaten before we left", Charles said.

"I don't think that's it", Janey said. The bus came to a halt.

"Eiffel Tower", the recording on the bus said.

Several people got up and exited the bus. When Bailey turned to leave, she caught the driver's eye once more. For just a moment, she thought she heard a distant scream, but shook it off and thanked him for the ride. The driver let the bus linger in the lot for a moment longer than usual, staring blatantly after the young woman who had just exited. He looked in the rearview mirror at an older gentleman and the gentleman winked at him as he nodded back.

Chapter 16

"Nothing", Janey said.

"Me too", Bailey said. They stood side by side looking up at the tower. They had walked around the base of the tower together, slowly, letting themselves absorb anything they could.

"That just can't be", Charles the Second said. "How can you feel something so strongly thousands of miles away, and now that you're here, nothing?"

"I don't know", Janey said. "I thought for sure that this was the answer."

"Me too", Bailey said. "Gertrude said it was the answer."

"Come on", Charles said. "Let's go sit and rest a while. You both look exhausted."

They found a shady spot near the base of the tower in a grassy knoll. The women sat down on the grass slowly, leaning against a large oak tree.

"A lot of this wasn't here before, was it Honey?" Charles the Second said.

"They've built a lot since the 70's and 80's", Janey said. "I'm thirsty. Sweetheart...?"

"I'm on it", her husband said.

"Can I get you a drink too?" Charles said, taking Bailey's hand.

"Water would be really nice, thank you", she replied.

The men strolled off a little ways towards the vendors. Both of the women sighed dejectedly and leaned further back against the tree.

"Tell me about Paris back then", Bailey said.

"Oh my", Janey said. "Well, it's almost puts you in mind of old school Hollywood. Do you know what I mean?"

"I think so", Bailey said. "So it was glamourous?"

"Exactly. Glamorous." Janey looked up at the tower. "I remember men in suits and the women were dressed to the nine's. Silks and furs. Satin and lace. They strolled around the tower, looking picture perfect. The air was thick with love. It was refreshing. "

"Did you see many of *us* at that time?" Bailey said, closing her eyes.

"A few", Janey said. "We weren't discriminated against as heavily over here. The French were much more accepting." Janey felt a prick on the back of her neck.

"Ow", Bailey said.

"Don't tell me you can feel my pain now also", Janey said as she reached to her neck to rub it.

"I just felt a prick on my..." Bailey said and never finished.

"Dear?" Janey said as she reached for Bailey. Suddenly everything went very dark as Janey felt the grip on she had Bailey's hand loosen.

Charles looked over at his father. "When do you think this will be over?" he said, grabbing the drinks.

"I pray soon", his father said. "I'm worried about your mother."

"Me too", Charles said. They made their way back over to the tree to find the women gone.

"Are they walking around the base of the tower again?" Charles the Second said.

"I'll check", Charles said. As he started toward the tower, his cell phone rang with the caller id of 'MOM'.

"This is Mom calling now", Charles said. "Mom!" he answered. "Where are you? We're..." Before he could finish the caller interrupted.

"I'd listen carefully if I were you", the voice said. Charles motioned to his father and put the call on speaker.

"You have my attention", Charles said, seething. As much as he wanted to scream and show emotion, he felt right away that it wouldn't help. "Where are my mother and fiancée?"

"Congratulations, then", the voice said with evil chuckle. "Perhaps you keep a better eye on her next time, no?"

"If you've hurt…" Charles started. His father looked up and tried to motion for a policeman.

"I thought you were smarter than that", the voice said. "No police", he said firmly.

"He's watching us", Charles said.

"That's right", the voice said.

"What do you want?" Charles the Second asked.

"I thought I was seeing things", the man's voice said. "My old eyes are getting tired. I thought to myself, it couldn't be. Jane. My sweet Jane. She's a little older, to be sure, but time has been kind to her. Not so much to you, Charles."

"Do I know you?" Charles the Second said. "Who are you?"

"You probably wouldn't remember a poor man like me. I mean you and Jane came to Paris, what, every March and September, right?" the voice snickered with disdain. "Twice a year for many years. You stopped making those trips, about 26 years ago, no?"

Charles covered the phone with his hand. "That's when I was born. How does this man know you, Dad?"

"I don't know", Charles the Second said. He removed his son's hand. "What is it that you want?"

"Oh it's rather simple. I want Jane. The other one, well, I'm not going to keep her long. My son, however..." His voice caught in his throat with a laugh that sent goosebumps breaking out all over Charles.

"If you touch her..." Charles began.

"I do believe I told you to listen carefully at the beginning", the voice beckoned. "I'm not sure what you brought you back here, Charles, but I thank you. I thank you for bringing her back to me. My Jane. The one I had before her, well it just wasn't the same."

Charles had never seen his father turn this shade of red. "So help me God..."

"So help you God indeed", the man's voice said. "You have three days to find her. The both of them. Although, if my calculations are correct, you'll find the young lady first, after my son is done. C'est la vie, Charles. Au revoir."

Chapter 17

"What the hell, Dad!?" Charles said, pacing back and forth. "No police? How are we supposed to find them? If he hurts Mom or Bailey..."

"I know what I'm about to say is going to sound crazy, but I'm not overly worried about your mom and Bailey right now." He held up his hand as his son was about to try to interrupt. "Kidnapping rule number one: you don't call and taunt if they're already dead or seriously hurt. He said no police. He never said anything about..." Charles the Second picked up his phone and hit the incognito button. He made sure the call he was about to place wouldn't be traced.

"Please tell me you're calling Francis", Charles said, pacing.

"I am", Charles the Second said. "Francis Bartlett please", he said when the secretary answered. "Francis?"

"Charles Wentworth? Is that you? Well I'll be a monkey's..."Francis answered.

"Save the pleasantries, Frank, we got trouble." Charles the Second began to pace and speak very fast.

"Okay, okay, slow down. First, where are you?" Francis said.

"Paris, France", he said slower.

"Well, by your tone I'm going to guess it's not for pleasure. Now, what happened?" Francis started to pack his briefcase as he listened to the details given by his friend about the sudden disappearance of his wife and soon-to-be daughter-in-law and headed out the door. He tapped his secretary on the shoulder after he shut his door.

"Lucy, forward all my calls to the answering service and cancel my meetings until further notice." Francis said, giving her a look that Lucy instantly understood.

"Yes, Mr. Bartlett, Sir", Lucy said, as she began to type furiously.

"Okay Charles, I'm on the next flight. I'll be there in a few hours", Francis said. "Just try to remain calm, and get to the embassy as inconspicuously and as soon as possible."

"We're on our way to the hotel, and then we'll get a shuttle bus", Charles the Second said.

"No Dad!" Charles said.

"What?" Charles the Second asked, covering the receiver of the cell phone.

"Let me speak to Charlie", Francis said. Charles got on the phone and Francis took a breath.

"What did you see?" Francis said.

"When we got on the shuttle bus to get to the tower, Bailey had a very strange reaction to seeing the driver", Charlie said.

"Okay", Francis said. "I know about your mother, but are you saying your fiancée is the same way?"

"If not stronger, Frank", he said.

"We'll start with the shuttle companies. I'm on my way. Hang tight, Kid", Frank said. "Try to keep your father calm", he said. As he got in his car and sped off, a flash of the FBI symbol was all that could be seen in the blur.

"I think it's working the other way around", Charles said, as he hung up and his father embraced him.

"It's going to be alright", his father said. "I know it will."

Bailey awoke and the smell of mildew was almost overwhelming. The floor was damp and dirty; it felt like she was sitting on the ground. The place she was in was dark. It took a while for her eyes to adjust. Strangely, she didn't feel scared, more like anxious, as if she was anticipating something. She noticed her surroundings were eerily quiet. As her eyes continued to adjust, she could make out some of her surroundings. In the corner was a table with straps on it, probably leather. There was a work bench to the right, and a small lamp on it. She felt around the ground next to her and began to panic. Where was Janey?

A tall figure entered the room from the back far right. He walked straight over to the work bench and turned on the lamp. The small room was suddenly flooded with a dim light and slowly she could start to make out the man who sat down. Even in the semi-dark, she could tell he was blonde and his cheek had a small scar on it.

"It's you! The bus driver!" Bailey screamed.

The man looked over at her and smiled. "You're woke up! Oh good! I was almost tired of waiting."

"What do you want with me?" Bailey said. "Where is the woman who was with me?"

"She's up at the house with Father", he said matter-of-factly. "I did good", he said to himself softly.

"What?" Bailey asked.

"I did good", he said, triumphantly. "Father said if I got him another one, I could keep one too."

"Keep one? Keep one of what?" Bailey asked.

"A girl", he said, grinning at her. "I can keep you."

Bailey tried to steady her breathing. "What are you going to do to me?"

"We're going to play!" the man said. At that statement, he got up and walked over to where Bailey was. He crouched down in front of her and smiled. "Do you want to play with me? We could play a game. I have lots of games!" he said excitedly.

Bailey shook her head no violently. The man stood, straightened up, and his demeanor gained and air of anger very quickly.

"You're being mean", he said, as he advanced on her and picked her up. "I don't like mean people."

Janey looked around the room. Somehow the room looked familiar, as if she had visited it before. She looked around at the comfortable furniture and the bed that she sat on was soft. It was beautifully decorated and she couldn't shake the feeling that she knew where she was. Aside from her hands and feet being bound, she was otherwise unscathed. She felt her stomach churn thinking of where Bailey must be.

An older gentleman entered the room and smiled at her. For a moment he stood perfectly still and just stared at her.

"I still can't believe it", he said. He walked slowly over to the chaise lounge next to the bed and sat down. "I just can't believe it."

"Believe what?" Janey said.

"That you're here; that I get to see you again." He leaned forward a bit. Janey could see his skin was weather worn. His hands were severely calloused and the sunspots on his forehead were plentiful.

"Remind me of how we know each other, Dear", Janey said, shifting her weight around in the bed.

"I doubt you'd remember me", he said. "But I remember you. You and your husband came to Paris every year when you were younger, no? I remember it well, every March and September. Every new bloom and every autumn."

"My favorite seasons", Janey said. "That much I remember, but I'm having a hard time placing you."

"As I said, I doubt you'd remember me. People like you don't remember the hired help", he snarled.

"I'll have you know, if I had properly met you, I would probably remember you. It doesn't matter to me what you do for a living." Janey shifted her weight again. "Also, I'd like to point out; I'm under a tremendous amount of stress being bound like this and separated from my daughter."

"She's fine and she's not your daughter. She's your daughter-in-law, soon to be. Well", he chuckled, "maybe." The man reached into a drawer on the nightstand. "Do you remember her?" He handed her the picture roughly.

"I know who she is now", Janey said, recognizing Gertrude from her dream and dropping the picture.

"Perhaps, if you saw her in her more 'natural habitat', he said. He grabbed one more picture and handed it to her.

Chapter 18

"That's me", she said, looking at the picture closely. In the picture she stood next to a shapely, lighter skinned woman in a waitress' uniform as they smiled at the photographer. The closer she looked at the picture, the more her memories started to come back.

"Madame, Monsieur", Gertrude said as she led Charles and Janey to a table in the back.

"Oui!" Janey said with a giggle. She was moving tentatively, so much that Charles placed his arm around her and helped her to sit.

"Thank you, Honey", Janey said, accepting the kiss he placed.

"Is everything well?" Gertrude said.

"Perfect", Charles the Second said. "This pretty lady is going to make me a father!"

"Well bravo!" Gertrude said. "This calls for a croissant on the house!" she said to Janey with a wink.

"You're too kind", Janey said.

"She was kind to me", Janey said. "She gave me excellent advice on morning sickness. I remember taking the picture because she told me I looked like royalty." Janey smiled bitterly. "I wish I had gotten to know her better."

"I did", the man said.

"You'll have to forgive me, but I don't like talking to someone and not knowing their name", Janey said.

"Well, I suppose you should know my name, considering we have the rest of our lives together." He took a deep breath. "My name is George."

"Robert Cavanaugh", Francis said. When he'd arrived in France, Francis immediately went straight to the embassy. The next morning when he saw the father-son pair, his heart broke. He embraced the younger Charles and stood with his arm around the elder Charles. "I've already contacted the police here and Interpol is involved. We're going to get them back, I promise."

"Who is Robert Cavanaugh?" Charles said.

"Robert Cavanaugh is the name of the shuttle driver", Francis said. "We'll get an address and find out everything we can before we go there."

"I have a feeling it's not going to be that simple", Charles the Second said. "The man said we have three days to find them. We only have a day and a half left now."

"I agree, but right now, Robert is the best lead we have" Francis said. "We'll get Janey and Bailey back, you have my word."

"What are you doing?" Bailey screamed as he put her on the table. The man stayed silent as he went about strapping Bailey down to the table. He hummed a slow tune softly as he tightened each leather strap around her ankles, torso, and shoulders.

"Please", Bailey said. "Please let me go."

"I can't", the man said. "I have to finish the job first."

"What job?" Bailey said, her voice faltering a bit.

"I have to finish the other woman and then I can be with you", he said, grabbing a pillow for her head.

"What's your name?" Bailey said, as she watched him turn to walk out. In her mind it suddenly clicked; the longer she kept him here, the longer that other woman had. Bailey thought about the 'her' they were supposed to save. Perhaps this was the 'her'. "What's your name?" she repeated.

The man stopped walking and turned to face Bailey. Close in the light she could see his face more clearly. The scar on his cheek wasn't the only mark he had.

"Bobby", he said softly.

"Bobby, did your father hurt you?" Bailey asked.

"I messed up", he said, solemnly. "But...but he loves me. Father says no one will ever look out for me like he does."

"Bobby, parents aren't supposed to hurt their children", Bailey said. "They are supposed to love them and take care of them. What he's doing isn't right."

"You're wrong!" Bobby said angrily. "He does love me! He's all I have now!"

"It's okay, it's okay", Bailey said. "You said you wanted to play a game. What kind of game?"

"You said no", Bobby said quietly.

"I was scared. I've been on the floor in the cold all night and I was scared. I'm alright now," Bailey said.

"Really?" Bobby said. He rushed over to her quickly. He undid the straps but left her hands bound. "I have cards and I have jacks. I like jacks."

"I like jacks too", Bailey said. Bobby turned his back and went to the work bench. She silently said a prayer and sent thoughts to Janey, praying she could hear her, or at least feel her. *"I'm alright"*, she repeated in her head like a mantra. *"Janey, I'm alright."*

"George", Janey repeated after him. Suddenly a powerful vibe went through her and she felt more at ease. Wherever Bailey was, she was okay. "What do you mean 'the rest of our lives'?"

"Just what I said. For years, I've been trying to replace you, trying to find someone that could be you. The moment I saw you all those years ago, well, I knew you were perfect for me. I prayed for your return every year. I even changed my trash route to the street where that café was you loved so much." He sat closer to her. "I thought I had found it with her", George said motioning to the picture, "but she wasn't right. None of them have been right. This last one was all wrong. She'll be a thing of the past soon enough. My son will see to that."

"What makes you think I'm going to stay here with you?" Janey said.

"You'll have no choice. Tis' your life, or your son's life. It is, as they say, very simple. Agree to stay, and your husband and son can leave the country; no hurt or harm will come to them. Say no, and well, I won't be responsible for the tragedy awaits them."

"I don't negotiate", Janey said firmly. "I'm not staying here."

"Hmm, I thought as much." George got up and walked over to the door. "Get comfortable. You're not going anywhere." He walked out the door leaving Janey still sitting on the bed, bound. George grabbed his keys and headed to the front door. When he heard screams from the basement, he sighed happily. "One down, one more to go", he said aloud.

Chapter 19

"We have the address now, what are we waiting for? Let's go!" Charles said impatiently.

"Not so fast, Kid", Francis said. "We have to be delicate about this. According to his file, Robert may not be the sharpest tool in the shed, but you can bet anything his father is. He's going to be expecting us. He's not stupid enough to think you guys hadn't come here, or even gotten the police involved. I'll bet you any money he's in the area, waiting to spot you coming out of here and taunt you with another phone call."

"So how then?" Charles said.

"Very quietly. Some plain clothes police are going to leave in a little while, looking a lot like tourists, and ride past the address. Some are already outside, canvassing the area." Francis put his hand on Charles' shoulder. "Trust me, this will work."

Another scream could be heard from the basement, as the ball rolled away again.

"You're really good!" Bobby said excitedly, as he brought the ball back to where she sat.

"I'd be better out of these ties", Bailey said, holding up her still bound hands.

"I can't", Bobby said. "You'll run away."

"No, I won't", Bailey said, shaking her head.

"Maybe later", Bobby said. "After I finish the other lady. Oh no!" he said, getting up suddenly. "Father will be angry if I don't finish!"

"It's okay", Bailey said, trying to calm him down.

"No! It's not okay! He'll be angry, and, and, he'll get the knife again!" Bobby started pacing furiously.

"It's okay", Bailey said. "I heard the door close a little while ago. I think he left."

"Really?" Bobby said, his demeanor lightening a bit. "Do you think we can play again?"

"Sure", Bailey said. "Would it be okay, if I had some water first?"

"Okay", he said as he went to the corner and grabbed a bottle of water from the counter. Bailey opened it and drank deeply.

"Thank you, Bobby. That was very nice of you", Bailey said. The small appraisal was met with a gigantic smile as he sat down again and grabbed the jacks and ball.

"You can go first this time", he said, handing the items to Bailey.

George sat on the park bench and watched the front of the Embassy. He knew the men were inside and as soon as he had his confirmation, he'd go back and finish the job.

Two men came out first and then a lovey-dovey couple. The woman giggled as her boyfriend whispered in her ear.

"Be advised of the man on the bench at 3 o'clock", the officer said into his girlfriend's earpiece.

"We got him", Francis said. George got up and started to move.

"He's moving", the female officer said, as she looked lovingly at her partner.

"Hold your position. I put a tail on him", Francis said.

"Roger that, at the ready", another officer in a car said.

George drove back to his house slowly. He took backstreets and even circled around the block several times. When he looked behind him, there were no cars following. Being lulled into a false sense of security, he parked in front of his home and paid no attention to the unmarked car parked a few car lengths away.

Getting out, he went in the house and directly to the back of the house. He opened the door to the study and instantly his anger rose. A shapely black woman was still bound and gagged in the chair, looking positively frightened.

"Bobby!" George screamed at the top of his lungs.

"Oh no!" Bobby said getting off the floor quickly. "Father is so angry with me!"

"Bobby! You hear me calling you!" George bellowed through the halls and down the stairs to the basement. The police and Francis surrounded the house, making a soft entry in. They walked quickly through the first level and when they reached the study, quickly undid the woman's restraints.

"Shhh", Francis said to her as they got her up. "We're going to get you help."

"Thank you", the woman cried. A female officer led her out and got her to the waiting paramedics.

The officers continued their search until they reached the bedroom where Janey was.

"Francis!" Janey said as he came over and gave her a quick hug.

He started to undo her restraints. "Are you hurt?" Francis asked.

"No. I was drugged slightly and put in this room." Francis helped Janey off the bed. "This room", Janey said remembering. "I saw it in my dreams. This is where he held Gertrude. "

"We'll have forensics tear this place apart Janey but we need to get you to Charles. He's waiting outside."

Francis handed Janey over to one of the officers. "No. I need to make sure Bailey is okay."

Francis instructed the officer to stay with Janey as they searched the rest of the house.

Chapter 20

"I'm so sorry, Father", Bobby said, as his father took out his pocket knife and swiped at his face. "I'm sorry."

"You *are* sorry! A sorry excuse for a son! I told you", he said, emphasizing each word with a cut to Bobby, "to take care of her first! I didn't care what you did with this one", he said motioning to Bailey. George straightened up. "No matter. Go ahead. Finish this one. We're going to have to leave soon. I have a feeling the police will be here shortly." He shoved the knife in Bobby's hand. "Go ahead."

"I can't, Father. She's my friend!" Bobby dropped the knife.

"Your *friend?* You don't have friends! Nobody wants you! Nobody will ever love you! Look at you! Even your mother didn't want to have anything to do with you!" George grabbed the knife and ran towards Bailey.

"No!" Bobby yelled, and his yell mixed with Bailey's scream as he ran and pushed his father out the way.

"That came from the basement", Francis said. The officers ran down the stairs following Francis in time to see George advance on Bobby with his knife.

"George Cavanaugh, drop your weapon!" Francis said. A team of officers surrounded him as he lunged toward his son. Francis pulled his trigger and shot George in the leg.

"Father!" Bobby screamed, as two police officers grabbed him and handcuffed him.

They got the restraints off of Bailey. "Bailey, I'm Francis, a friend of Charles. You're going to be okay. Are you hurt?"

"Where's Janey?" she said.

"Janey is just fine", Francis said. "She's waiting outside for you."

"Is the other woman OK?" Bailey asked.

"She will be, hopefully." He led her up the stairs to where Janey was waiting.

"Bailey!" Janey said, grabbing the young woman and placing her in a death grip hug. "Are you okay, Dear? I'm so sorry. This is all my fault."

"Stop that", Bailey said, coming out of the hug. "I'm fine. Bobby is mentally challenged; I'm almost positive of that. We spent most of the time playing jacks. I figured the longer I played along, the more time that woman had."

"So smart", Janey said. She hugged Bailey once more. "I want to go home."

"Me too", Bailey chimed in.

The two women were escorted out the house into the waiting arms of the men who loved them. Hugging each other, tears flowed and comfort was given. While George was taken away in the ambulance, Bobby was taken away in squad car.

"What's going to happen to Bobby?" Bailey said.

Francis sighed. "Unfortunately he has to be charged for the crimes he committed but because of his mental status, they can't put him in a general population prison. I'm petitioning for an asylum."

"He saved my life. His father was going to stab me." Bailey hugged close to Charles. "His father abused him so much."

"The analyst back at Interpol had gotten some more on that. It seems that Bobby is the offspring of victim number 3." Francis shook his head. "That kid never had a chance."

An officer came out the house shaking his head.

"What you got, Bill?" Francis asked.

The officer shook his head again. "It looks like the little lady was right. We're only just on the main floor and we've found the remains of what seems to be at least five victims. It's going to take forensics at least a week to start identifying these women."

Francis looked at Bailey and Janey. "I should hire you two. You just unearthed probably one of the most prolific serial killers in France."

"Don't care", Bailey said as she buried her head in her fiancé's chest. "I just want to go home."

"Me too, Dear", Janey said, as they were led to squad cars and back to the Embassy to take statements.

Chapter 21

With the statements taken, the foursome wearily left the Embassy to head back to the hotel with Francis. While Francis fretted over Janey and Bailey's decision to forgo a hospital trip, he also understood.

"At least promise me you'll go see your doctor and get a blood test when you get back to states", Francis said.

"I'll make sure of it", Charles the Second said.

"Are you guys going to leave now?" Francis said, hugging the elder Charles.

"Our flight is due to leave tomorrow morning, so we're just going to stay in the hotel tonight and leave in the morning."

Francis turned to Bailey. "I hope you can come back soon. I don't want this to be your only memory of this place. France can be beautiful and intriguing, just like a woman. It's a shame this had to happen on your first trip."

"I'm sure I'll be back, but for now, I want to forget about this for a while." Bailey yawned deeply. "If it's all the same, I think I'll just take a shower and lie still for a while."

"Of course", Francis said, giving her a quick hug. "It's been a pleasure, Bailey."

"Really?" Bailey chuckled. "Really? A pleasure?" The foursome looked at Francis and laughed.

"Oh, you know what I meant", Francis said.

After Bailey left, Janey went to her adjourning room to follow suit. She finished her shower and dressed quickly. She went in to check on Bailey only to find her fast asleep.

Janey sat down on the bed next to her, fully expecting to sit next to and just comfort the young woman, and found herself in a deep sleep very quickly.

"What are you doing here?" Bailey said, turning around and seeing Janey approaching through the trees.

"No idea", Janey said. "I supposed I just followed you." She stood silent with Bailey for a few minutes. Is this forest behind the property?"

"I do believe so", Bailey said.

"Well, who are we waiting for?" Janey said.

"I'm not sure, but I have a feeling we shouldn't leave." Bailey looked at Janey and burst out in deep laughter. "So we can do this together now, huh?"

"Nothing surprises me anymore", Janey said. "Since I've met you, nothing and everything has made sense. You know", Janey said looking off in the distance, "I've been keeping something from you."

"You don't say?" Bailey said, turning to Janey with a surprised expression on her face.

"I knew you had been visiting the grounds for some time. I had to keep it quiet. I felt you before I even saw you." Janey looked at the ground. "I knew something big was coming, I just had no idea what it was going to be." She grabbed Bailey's hand. "Are you angry with me, Dear?"

"Not at all", Bailey said, squeezing her hand.

"Look, Dad", Charles said as he peeked in on the duo sleeping. "They're holding hands." He laughed. "Mom gets to sleep with my fiancée before I do."

Charles the Second chuckled and bit and then scrunched his face up in deep concentration. "I wonder", he said as he watched his wife and his soon-to-be daughter-in-law hold hands and fidget in their sleep.

"You don't think they're dreaming together, do you?" Charles said.

"I think that whatever this is", his father answered, "they have to see it through. Perhaps this is the end. If so, I, for one, am very grateful. I've had enough excitement for more than one lifetime."

The two Charles' went into the second room. "Maybe we should order a light dinner, you know, for when they wake up." Charles said.

"You're hungry, aren't you?" he father said with a raised eyebrow.

"Starving!" Charles said, picking up the menu.

"Perhaps we should walk ahead a bit", Janey said.

Bailey and Janey took a few steps and when she heard a twig snap under her foot, she stopped.

"Why did you....?" Janey began when she saw what Bailey saw.

"You know", Gertrude said, "you two are really something else." The glowing orb shaped in Bailey great aunt's likeness came closer to Janey. "Thank you for remembering me."

"I'm sorry I didn't earlier", Janey said. "Please forgive me. My age and all."

"Nonsense. You're still as spry as ever." Gertrude turned to look at Bailey. "You're still skinny", Gertrude said. "You need to fix that."

"I'll try", Bailey said with a smile. She became solemn. "I'm so sorry about what happened to you."

"I didn't suffer too much. Just know", Gertrude said, choking up, "I'll be forever grateful to you, the both of you."

"I'm glad we were able to save that woman", Bailey said.

"You did so much more than that", Gertrude said. "You've brought peace to so many families; to our family, Bailey. My mother can rest in peace and now, so can I." She started to dissipate when Janey called her name.

"So how does this work?" Janey asked. "Will Bailey and I continue to be connected like this? Can we dream together? Can we..."

Gertrude interrupted. "I don't know, Doll. For all we know, this may very well end when you two awake. It may continue. You were brought together for a reason. One part of the reason is over." She looked to Bailey. "Another reason just may present itself. These things..."

"...are often unpredictable, at best!" Bailey finished, as she looked up in awe. "My dad used to tell my mom that all the time."

"He was right, Doll. Keep doing what you're doing", Gertrude said as she vanished. "Some things need to be discovered."

With that, the orb that was Gertrude disappeared leaving two women staring after her in awe.

"Whoa", Bailey said as she awoke.

Janey woke up a split second later. She looked at the young woman sitting next to her in the bed and smiled. "Hungry, Dear?"

Bailey smiled at Janey warmly. "So we're not even going to address what just happened?" Bailey said as she climbed out the bed and helped Janey down.

"No, we are not", Janey said. She smiled brightly. "You will keep studying the earth. I'll tell Charles to find another writer for Charlie's foundation. You have some very important work to do. Whatever you need; just let me know." She hugged the young woman. "You know, you can call me Mama too, if you like."

Bailey hugged her back tightly. "I like", she said, through a few tears.

Chapter 22

A few weeks later, Bailey sat next to her soon-to-be-husband and smiled happily as they tasted sample after sample of cake. The manor had been buzzing for a while now. The family kept as much of what could be kept under wraps about France. Still, a good bit of it got out. Stories floated around about the Virginia heroines who saved the captured woman in Paris and even though Bailey and Janey turned down interviews daily, they did however elect to do one interview, and decidedly left out the paranormal connection, saying that they had "a special inside track".

The town buzzed for quite some time, but then a new buzz surfaced. The wedding of the year was happening very soon. Bailey was so busy that the only time she had to get back to the forest and meditate was in the dead still of the night, when Charles would usually come and walk a very sleepy Bailey back to the house.

Bailey still stayed in the main house in her room, but spent many hours with Charles putting her own touches in his, now "their" wing. New drapes and hints of purple everywhere made her feel more at home when she was there. It was during one of these times that their honeymoon was mentioned again.

"Tell me you gave it some more thought", Charles said as he handed her the screw driver. Upgrading from a full sized bed to a king was definitely a two man job or at least a one man, one woman job.

"What am I supposed to be thinking about?" Bailey said distractedly as she screwed in the last screw on the bottom base. "Tell me again why we went with wrought iron?"

"It's classic and it has got great support", Charles said looking up at her. If Bailey followed suit, a very deep blush would be creeping up around her neck soon.

"Just what do you plan on doing in this bed?" Bailey said, the blush in her face becoming very pronounced.

"Oh nothing", Charles said, chuckling. "Now tell me, where do you want to go?"

"Not Paris", Bailey said. As much as she had been able to let of a lot of the bad feelings associated with the city go, she wasn't in a hurry to return.

"Well that's for sure", Charles said. He grabbed the headboard. "Hand me the drill."

Bailey grabbed the drill. "Okay. How about Brazil?"

Charles stopped drilling. "Brazil?"

"You're going to think I'm weird", Bailey said.

"I already do", Charles said, ducking from Bailey's punch. "Careful, I have a drill and I'm not afraid to use it! Now tell me!" he said, playfully pointing the drill at her.

"I want to be the Girl from Ipanema", Bailey said softly.

"What?" Charles said.

"I want to be the Girl from Ipanema!" Bailey practically shouted. "I want to hear that song as I walk along the beach. I want to wear the pretty swim suit with the sarong flowing around my legs. I want my hair blowing in the soft summer-like wind and feel..."

"Feel...?" Charles said.

"Absolutely beautiful", Bailey said.

"You are!' Charles said, putting down the drill and walking over to her. He wrapped his arms around her. "You know I think you're the most beautiful woman in the world, right?"

"Thank you for saying it out loud", Bailey said, "but this is a fantasy I've always had. It's silly, I know..."

"It is", Charles said with a small laugh. "But it's you and I think it's a great idea. We could see the sights. I always wanted to see the Cristo Redentor."

"Then we're going to Brazil?" Bailey asked excitedly.

"We're going to Brazil!" Charles said. He watched happily as his bride-to-be bounced around the room excitedly. When she made her way back to him, he spun her around in a twirl and as they stood face to face, electricity surging through them, they shared a kiss that could have nearly blown out every circuit in the house.

"Ahem", a voice said from behind them. "I didn't realize kissing was the way to put a bed together", Janey said in a bemused voice.

"Hi Mama", Bailey and Charles said in unison.

"Hi yourselves", Janey said. "What are we celebrating?" she said. "I heard the yelps from out in the main hall."

"We picked a honeymoon spot!" Bailey said.

"Well...?" Janey said.

"Brazil!" Charles said.

"How lovely!" Janey said. "Actually, that was one of the reasons I was looking for you two. The other was about the ceremony."

"Oh?" Bailey said.

"Well, the pastor wants to know if you're doing your own vows or the traditional ones", Janey asked.

"I don't think we even thought of that", Charles said. "Well if it's not broke, don't fix it, right? Traditional ones sound good."

"Then it's settled", Janey said as she turned to walk out.

"Wait a minute", Bailey said. "What if I want to say a thing or two?"

"Is it really necessary?" Charles said. "We know how we feel about each other. Why do we need to tell everyone?"

"We're telling each other too!" Bailey said.

"Bailey", Charles said. "We don't have to stand in front of everyone and say how we feel. We know."

"Do we?" Bailey said.

"Why is this such a big issue for you? I don't need to confess all my deepest emotions to you in front of everyone. You know I love you."

"Just like I knew you thought I'm beautiful", Bailey said. "It's okay, Charles", Bailey said. She walked past Janey and planted a small kiss on her soon-to-be mother-in-law's cheek. "I'm going to go for a short drive."

"I'll join you", Charles said.

"Not necessary", Bailey said as she walked out the door.

Chapter 23

"Please help me understand this", Charles said as he sat in the library with his father. Janey had filled Charles the Second in on the disagreement as soon as he got in.

"Take a seat, Son", his father said. He swirled his liquid around in his glass and took a small sip. "Did you know that Bailey has her vows written already?"

"No, I didn't". Charles said. "She does? Really?"

"Really. She'd kill me if she knew I was telling you this. She...confides in me sometimes. We walk around the grounds in the late afternoons sometimes. We look at the horses; talk about her past. The night you proposed, she began writing."

"Dad..." Charles started.

"Listen", his father said, interrupting. "I know it's not easy to put into words exactly what you feel, but on your wedding day, you have a very rare gift. There will be days in your life where you're running around like a chicken with your head cut off, excuse the expression. You have your work, Bailey has her research. When you have children, which your mother is hoping for really soon, you'll be a dad and a businessman and a husband. On your wedding day, you have the very rare gift of having each other's undivided attention."

"I say I love you to her all the time", Charles said.

"Then your phone goes off, you're running to the office, or it's dinner time, or she's headed to the forest or library", Charles the Second said. "Take the time, Son. There will be times in your marriage that you will be so busy, so exhausted or just plain distracted to give each other the time and affection you each deserve. Use this opportunity to tell her in no uncertain terms what she is to you; how much she means to you, because there will be times when she'll think back and remember that day and take comfort in no matter how busy you get, you confessed and professed to her exactly what she does for you. You took the time to tell her that she is your everything." Charles the second took another drink. "Unless she's not your everything."

"Of course she is!" Charles said. "It's just...I'm not good at this, Dad."

"Yes you are", his father said. "All have you do is remember those kisses you share, and how you feel when you look in her eyes, and the words will come tumbling out."

Bailey grabbed the keys to the Sebring and hopped in. Before she could even start the ignition, she heard the passenger door open and close.

"Well, you look positively livid!" the passenger said, buckling her seatbelt.

"Mary?" Bailey said, leaning over and hugging the woman. "I thought you wouldn't be in until tomorrow!"

"We got in a little while ago. I went upstairs to look for you, but Mama said you'd probably be out here", Mary said. "Now, why are you absolutely livid?"

"Your brother..."Bailey started.

"Oh that can't be good. It's never good when you refer them as a title rather by name", Mary said. "You guys are so simpatico. What could he have done?"

"It's not really what he's done, it's what he doesn't want to do", Bailey said, fidgeting with the car gears.

"Is this...sensitive stuff?" Mary said, tentatively. "Even though I think of you as a sister, I don't think I'm prepared to talk about my little brother's..."

"No, no, nothing like that", Bailey said with a slight chuckle. "It's about our wedding vows."

"Okay, what about them?" Mary asked.

"He won't write any", Bailey said with a sigh. "He thinks the traditional ones are just perfect."

"And you want something more heartfelt?" Mary asked.

"I would love that. Don't get me wrong, I know he loves me. When we kiss, it's electrifying. I feel safe with him. But…oh maybe he's right", Bailey said, dropping her head into her waiting hands.

"Let me get this straight. You feel loved, and you know he loves you, but you want to know to what extent?" Mary said.

"That sounds about right", Bailey said.

"Hmm", Mary said.

"I know that 'Hmm', Mary. "Okay, let me have it", Bailey said.

"Alright, but remember, you asked for it." Mary cleared her throat. "I'm in agreement with my brother."

"Really?" Bailey said.

"Do you know another guy who would go to France to dig up spirits of dead relatives, help rescue you, walk you back from the forest when you fall asleep, and yes I know about that, my brother and I talk", Mary said. "Face it, Kid, you're a handful."

Mary looked at the shocked expression on Bailey's face and laughed. "A nice, sweet handful, but still." She smiled at Bailey. "Remember, you asked for it, Sis." She turned and faced Bailey. "Did you know that men and women define love differently?"

"Um", Bailey said.

"Don't let Mama hear you say that", Mary chuckled. "Bailey, my brother is head over heels in love with you. When he calls me, most of our conversations are about you."

"Really?" Bailey asked.

"Really. Tell me, why is this so important?" Mary asked.

"I suppose, well, I just want to hear it. Today, I told him a secret fantasy of mine. How it would make me feel beautiful. He told me that he thinks I'm beautiful." Bailey started to choke up a bit.

"Okay", Mary said.

"It was the first time he'd ever said it out loud", Bailey said. She let a deep sigh. "I guess it just felt good for him to say it out loud. I assumed it, but it felt so good to hear it. I am going to cherish that moment for the rest of my life."

"Really?" A voice said coming up on the passenger side. "I've never said that out loud?"

"I'm going to... just go and find Mama", Mary said, smiling and squeezing Bailey's hand. "You two need to talk." She got out of the convertible and hugged her brother. "Talk to her", she whispered in his ear.

Charles slid in the car. "Is that true? I never said that out loud?"

Bailey nodded as a small tear escaped her eye and slid down her cheek. Charles reached up and brushed it away, looking Bailey deep in her eyes.

"Can you forgive my omission of the obvious?" Charles said.

"Can you forgive my pushing you to do something you didn't want to?" Bailey countered.

"Bails", Charles started. "It's not that I don't want to, I'm just not the best at it. I felt, well, kind of embarrassed."

"I don't want to embarrass you", Bailey said. "Mary gave me a good talking to. I realized that she has a point. You showed me how beautiful I was on our engagement night. You rescued me in Paris, and you take care of me and all my weirdness."

"True", Charles said, "and you do things for me. You tell me I'm the best when I'm headed into a meeting. You compliment my choice in suits, you bring me mint tea when I'm stressed and you tell me how handsome I am all the time." He sighed a bit. "I can do the same for you. I should do the same for you and I will. Starting with these", he said, pulling out a small napkin paper from his pocket.

"What's this?" Bailey said, reaching for the napkin as Charles pulled it out of her grasp.

"These", he said waving the paper in front her teasingly, "are the beginnings of my vows. I'm not as far along as you, I know, but...oh, oops."

"As far along...Charles Alexander Wentworth the Third, what do you know?" Bailey said, crossing her arms seriously, all the while trying to hide her amusement.

"Okay, so don't kill Dad", he said.

"Papa!" she said in a huff. "Does he even know what 'confidence' means?"

"He was just trying to help", Charles said, "and he did, so..."

"So I'm not going to say anything", she said, relaxing her arms.

"I'm really sorry, Bailey. I don't like when you're upset with me." Charles said, timidly reaching for her hand.

"Me too", Bailey said, reaching for his embrace. She locked eyes with him, and for one moment the whole world stopped. Charles leaned in to kiss her softly and when their lips met, sparks flew.

Chapter 24

The morning of the wedding was a cool, crisp autumn day. The sun was bright and a few puffy white clouds lined the sky. Wentworth Manor was bustling with activity as Charles and Bailey prepared to say 'I do' in front of family and friends. A few of Bailey's cousins flew in from New York for the nuptials and the "royalty" of the town was in attendance.

The night before the ceremony, Bailey and Charles both opted out of respective parties, citing that they didn't need to celebrate leaving the single life.

"I'm moving on to a much better part of life", Charles said, eying Bailey sweetly.

"I agree. Besides, single life can be a bit lonely at times", Bailey said.

"You two", Mary said, sitting next to her husband Robert at the dinner table. "That's all fine and dandy, for now", said Mary shaking her head. "Wait 'til you have kids!"

"Oh boy", Robert said. "Here comes the 'before I was a mom' speech", he said chuckling.

"Oh come now", Mary said. "You make it sound like I loathe motherhood. I love my boys", she said, glancing over at the kiddie table. "But, in all honesty, there are days I long for the carefree days of just being a wife." She leaned close to Bailey and lowered her voice. "And single", she added with a devilish smile.

"I heard that", Robert said, chuckling softly and nudging her in the side, returning her kiss to him on the cheek.

"Wouldn't trade you for the world, Bob", Mary said.

"Me too", Bailey whispered to Charles, squeezing his hand under the table.

Now, with the manor in full swing, Bailey was starting to feel a bit overwhelmed. Everywhere she turned, someone was fussing over her: her dress, her hair, the food... When she saw her chance, she took a small moment and went out to the garden near the back of the house.

Bailey always loved to take lingering walks through the garden. It was like her very own secret paradise. The hanging branches of the Weeping Willows reminded of her being lost in a small jungle and the lush greenery was calming. There was water fountain in the corner that aided the overall feeling of peace and serenity.

Bailey sat on the small bench and looked at the Koi fish in the pond below the water fountain. She only jumped slightly when she heard approaching footsteps.

"I thought I'd find you out here", Janey said.

"Hi Mama", Bailey said, and instinctively slid over to make room for her Janey to sit down.

"Let me guess", Janey said, giving her a quick side hug. "Too much?"

"A little bit, yes", she said with a small smile. "It's just all so new. I've never had this much fuss made over me, not even from the cotillion."

"It can be a bit much", Janey said. She reached in her pocket. "Here", she said. "Take a small sip of this."

"One day you're going to tell me what's in this little bottle" Bailey said, taking the small vial from Janey.

"It's Valerian Root", she said. "Too much, and you're going right to sleep. A little sip or so, and you're relaxed."

"Hmm", Bailey said. She took a small sip. "Did you infuse this with mint?"

"Nicely done", she said, taking the vial back. "Yes, with chocolate mint leaves." She turned to the young woman.

"What?" Bailey said with a small giggle.

Janey reached up and let a few curly locks of Bailey's hair run over her fingers. The updo Bailey wore framed her oval shaped face. Her makeup was light, with just a touch of rose on the apple of her cheeks.

"I'm just remembering when I first met you. How much you've grown, and yet, how you've still remained the same", Janey said. "No worries. You're going to be in a beautiful dress and soon, you'll be Mrs. Wentworth, like me!" Janey stood up. "Take a few more minutes, but then do come back up. We can't have a wedding without a bride!"

Bailey watched the older woman walk away as she took a deep breath and steadied her nerves. "Mrs. Wentworth", Bailey said aloud. "I can't do this."

"Of course you can", was whispered into the small breeze that blew near Bailey's ear. She smiled nervously and got up, tentatively walking back up to the main house.

The Conservatory was beautifully decorated in autumn colors bringing the outside vibrancy of the season inside. The large room was split into two sections; golden high-back chairs with bright orange and forest green satin ribbons flowing from them in multiple rows sat facing the alter. Small trees lined the walls, gleaming softly with white lights, and adorned with bright orange and yellow leaves. The runner on the floor was a beautiful Eggshell color with the Wentworth 'W' monogram on it in a zigzag fashion. The arc at the altar was flowing with small with white peony flowers, green ivy, and sycamore leaves. The large windowed doors were ajar; the light from the slowly setting sun beaming in, basking the wedding goers in a velvety warmth.

A light and jaunty classical piece started and Charles Wentworth the Second walked his wife down the aisle to their seats. Dressed in a shimmering burnt sienna dress, Janey was every bit of the proud and beautiful mother of the groom. Not to be outdone, the elder Charles, with his vest and tie matching his beautiful wife, made the tuxedo he wore look as though the suit was made only for him.

As they took their seats, jazz version of 'You Were Meant for Me' played and Robert and Mary walked down the aisle, ready to take their places. A small fanfare was heard, and Charles Alexander Wentworth the Third came to the back doors. A singer stepped up to the side podium and began to sing a slow version of "I Was Made to Love Her."

As Charles walked down the aisle in his Black tuxedo and matching tie and cummerbund, a small tear threatened to fall from his right eye. He thought back to the first time he met Bailey; an intriguing woman trespassing on his property chasing the unknown. Almost a year later, he was here, about to make her his wife. 'So much has happened', he thought as he smiled at his sister and brother-in-law standing at the altar. He didn't even want to think about what his life would be like if he'd never met her. Taking his place at besides Robert, Charles nervously wrung his hands together as they waited for the signal for Bailey.

With the cue given, Bailey stood behind the closed double doors that would lead her into the Conservatory. On the other side of that door were her cousins, Charles's family, the Mayor, and some of the more prominent people of their town; people she'd grown to respect and adore. More importantly, on the other side of that door, her soon-to-be husband stood at the altar waiting for her. He'd be waiting on her to arrive, so they could profess their undying love to each other and say I do. The Wedding March began and as the doormen reached for either side of the double door to open them for her grand entrance; Bailey held out her hand and stopped them.

Chapter 25

"Miss?" the doorman said, his hand frozen on the handle. He looked up at the other doorman, curiosity plaguing his facial features.

"I, uh, I just need a minute", Bailey said, backing away from the double doors. She walked over to the staircase turning slightly as she passed the hall mirror. Bailey stared in the mirror for what must have seemed like hours. Her dress was simple, but elegant. Winter white lace flowed gently over the satin underneath; the neckline a beautiful sweetheart shaped. Her train was just at her feet and a sash of silk was wrapped around her waist, the flowers playing at her hips. Through the veil, she could see her small tiara; the curls around the nape of her neck and her forehead matching. Beautiful was not a strong enough word to describe what Bailey looked like. But for the pretty dress, the gorgeous shoes, and the glamourous hair, Bailey still felt out of place. She remembered the first night she spent in the house. She thought of the whirlwind events that lead to her adventures, romance and even some closure on her own life events. This house was enchanting and just a bit mysterious.

"Mom?" Charles said.

"I don't know, Charlie", Janey said. "When we spoke in the garden, she was fine. Well, not fine, but okay."

"I need to find her", Charles said.

"Let me go", Mary said. "I can talk to her, you know, woman, to woman."

"I think I'd better", Charlie said. "I think I know what this is about." He eyed his mother. "Don't worry, I won't look at her. I'll keep the tradition alive."

Charles turned to the audience. "Ladies and Gentlemen, thank you for your patience. There has been a slight, unforeseen delay, but we will continue within a moment's time." He slipped out the side door of the room and headed to the main hall.

"Bailey?" Charles said to the side.

"You can't see me!" Bailey said, hiding around the corner of the staircase.

"I'm aware", Charles said chuckling. "Are you alright? You missed your cue."

"I know", Bailey said in a sad voice. "I'm really sorry."

"It's okay", Charles said. "I bought us some time. So tell me, why did you miss the cue?" He came around the corner with his eyes closed, his hand reaching for hers. He sat on the lower step of the stairs and waited. A few moments later and a smaller hand enclosed his.

"Are your eyes closed too?" Charles asked.

"They are", Bailey said.

"OK then", Charles began, "tell me, what's on your mind? Does this have to do with your dad not being here?

"No", Bailey said, and smiled. It was just like Charles to be sensitive to the fact that his parents were sitting inside and hers weren't.

"I give", Charles said.

"Mrs. Wentworth", Bailey said softly.

"My mother?" Charles asked.

"No, me", Bailey said. "Am I Mrs. Wentworth material? Am I going to be a good wife for you? Can I really do this?" Bailey started to rock back and forth. "I'm good at being Bailey. I have been all my life. I'm good at being a girlfriend too, I think."

"You're an amazing girlfriend", Charles said.

"Thanks", Bailey said, "but being a wife! Can I even do that?"

Charles sat quiet for a while. "Hmm." he said.

"Hmm? That's it? Hmm?" Bailey retorted.

"Let me ask you one question. Can you love me?" Charles asked, squeezing her hand.

"I already do", Bailey said.

"Can you put up with me when I'm totally stressed out?" Charles said.

"I already do", Bailey said, with a chuckle.

"Can you comfort me when I'm sad?" Charles asked.

"Always", Bailey said, a small tear escaping her eye.

"Then you can be a wife. You just need to keep doing those things." He brought her hand to his lips. "I was scared too, Bails. I thought, 'could I even do this? Am I ready for a wife?' But this is us, Bailey. This wedding, the ceremony, it's just a formality. This day is about us. Our marriage. Our love for each other. You and me against the world and whatever it has in store for us." He stood up, shakily. "I'm going to be waiting for you. And you...?"

"Won't miss my cue", Bailey said, with a nervous giggle.

"That's my girl", Charles said.

"You know", Bailey said, eyes still closed and gently coming off the steps with the help of the doorman. "I never thought I'd ever have a real best friend. I'm glad it's the man who's about to be my husband." She let his hand go, as one of the doormen led him back to the side hall.

Charles walked into the Conservatory and stood next to Robert.

"Everything okay?" Robert said.

"She's perfect", Charles said. "Just when I think we can't have more in common, I find out we do."

The Wedding March began again, and when the minister announced to 'all rise' for the second time, the double doors opened to reveal a stunningly beautiful Bailey Matthews, bouquet in hand and ready to say I do.

Chapter 26

Bailey's walk down the aisle was slow and deliberate. With each step, it was getting harder and harder for Charles not to cry. Never in his life had he seen such a radiance of beauty. The dress was phenomenal; the hair and the veil, perfection. What set off the glow of light that surrounded Bailey was the smile she wore. He remembered the first time she smiled at him, in the forest. Her laugh triggered a release of emotion inside of him and when she looked in his eyes and smiled, his whole world was right.

Bailey never took her eyes off of him. As the sun set in behind him, a halo of light shone around his face, calling to her to him like a beacon. Every doubt and fear she ever had vanished; renewed within her was a love so strong it could move mountains.

Bailey handed her bouquet to Mary and stood before her groom, his hand engulfing hers.

"You are absolutely exquisite", Charles whispered to her.

"And you're breathtaking", Bailey replied.

"Dearly beloved", the minister began. "We are gathered here today, in the sight of God and man to join Bailey Marie Matthews and Charles Alexander Wentworth the Third in holy matrimony. The bonds of marriage are not to be taken lightly, but with a solemn heart and clear mind. Therefore", he continued. "Should there be any just cause as to why these two should not be lawfully joined as man and wife, let it be known now, or forever hold your peace."

The room was silent for a moment as Bailey and Charles waited with bated breath for something to happen. When more silence followed, they each breathed a sigh of relief.

"I had a sinking feeling that Charlotte would make an entrance", Bailey said.

"Me too", Charles countered. "Thank God for small miracles."

Janey sat back in her chair and smiled as she overheard that last remark. 'Small miracles', she thought. 'That was no small miracle. That 'miracle' as it were, took a call to the sheriff and having great security.' She chuckled a bit at her inner thoughts.

"What did you do?" Charles the Second whispered in her ear.

"What had to be done", Janey said, and kissed his cheek softly.

"The bonds of marriage are sacred", the minister said, calling Janey's attention back to the ceremony. "The couple has elected to say a few words to express themselves. Ms. Matthews, you may begin."

Bailey looked deep into the eyes of her love and pulled a small piece of paper from her tiny satchel. "I had originally written down all the things I love about you; about how kind you are and how sweet you are to me, all about how you make me feel. But now, I feel the need to speak from my heart." She took a deep breath.

"When I first met you, I felt a lot like I feel today. Scared, excited, nervous; those were just a few of the emotions overwhelming me then. Most of all, I felt anticipation. I felt as if something amazing was going to happen to me. It did. Over the time that I've gotten to know you, I've learned more about the world and myself than I could have ever imagined. You've taught me to trust my instincts, face my fears and open my heart. For that Charles, I will treasure you always. You are a guiding light for me, a safe haven and you make everyday a new adventure. Always know that I love you, beyond the words I can write, the thoughts I can think and the dreams I can dream. You are a part of my spirit now, and I will carry you in my heart, from now until the end of time. And maybe", she said winking, "even after." Bailey's last words elicited a small chuckle from the audience. She reached her hand up to Charles' face, and with a gloved finger, wiped a tear from his cheek.

"My son", the minister said. "I do believe it's your turn."

Charles pulled a napkin from his coat pocket. It was the same napkin that a while ago he grabbed and began to write his vows on.

"Is that the same...? Bailey asked with a smile.

"The very same", Charles said. He unfolded it and began. "A short time ago, I wrote one line down on this napkin. It reads, 'speak from your heart'." He folded it back up and handed it to Bailey. "I met you, on a cold, crisp evening, walking on my property and since then, my life has never been the same. In such a short time you went from being the mysterious girl who sought the unknown, to my girlfriend and then my fiancée. Somewhere in that time, you became my very best friend. If I may, I want to share a short story with you all."

Charles took his bride's hand and continued. "About three months into our relationship, Bailey and I took a pair of horses out for a walk. We had practiced in the stables before, but this was on a trail, in the evening. At first, it was fine, the horses were walking and we were just chatting, enjoying the night. A gopher…"

"I think it was a badger, Sweetie", Bailey said, interrupting.

"Okay, a *small* badger", Charles said, rolling in eyes mockingly, "startled Bailey's horse and she fell, landing in a thicket of bushes. She was fine, thank goodness, but I realized something that day; something that I carry with me always. When she fell, I leapt from my horse. I didn't care about my safety, I didn't care about where the horses went, I didn't care about the *'badger'*, he said, smirking at Bailey. "The only thing that mattered to me was you. You were my top priority. I cared more about you than my surroundings, my property, than anything. It was then I knew that I loved you. It was then I knew you were a part of my very being. When you breathe out, I breathe in. Bailey, you are so much a part of me that I can't remember my life before you. I love you, Bailey Marie Matthews. From the depths of my soul and from the part of me that I didn't even know existed. From now until forever, you have my heart and my spirit."

Janey and Charles the Second held each other close, listening to two people whose love rivaled theirs decree an undying love for each other. The audience fought back tears as the couple turned to the minister.

"May I have the rings, please?" the minister asked. Robert and Mary both handed the couple the rings they had been holding.

"Ms. Matthews, Mr. Wentworth, take your rings and place them on your partner's left ring finger", the minister stated.

Bailey shakily put the platinum band on Charles' hand and Charles slipped the diamond encrusted platinum band on Bailey's hand.

"Do you, Bailey and Charles", the minister stated, "promise to love, honor and obey each other? For better or for worse, in sickness and in health, wealth or poverty, promise to cleave only unto each other, and cherish each other for as long as you both shall live? If in accordance with these vows, confirm with and 'I do'."

Bailey looked deep into Charles' eyes. "I do", she said.

Charles smiled and gazed at Bailey. "I most certainly do", he said.

"Then", the minister declared, "By the power invested in me, by God and the state of Virginia, I now pronounce you man and wife. What God has joined together, let no man put asunder. Will you please bow a moment for prayer?"

The audience along with the wedding party bowed their heads.

"Heavenly Father, we come to you with a prayer for strength and longevity for the marriage of Bailey and Charles. Bless them, O Father, with patience and endurance, but most of all love, respect and forgiveness. In Christ's name we pray, Amen", the minister finished.

"Amen", the audience repeated.

The minister joined their hands as he lifted the veil for Bailey. "It is with great pleasure", the minister said with a gigantic smile, "to introduce for the first time and present to you, Mr. and Mrs. Charles and Bailey Wentworth." He turned to Charles. "You may now kiss your bride."

Charles smiled as he took Bailey in his arms. "I love you", he whispered.

"I love you", Bailey said. Bailey giggled slightly as Charles surprised her by dipping her lowly and kissed her deeply. The moment their lips touched, lighting lit up the darkening sky.

The couple stood in the receiving line with Charles' parents, and received many congratulations and well wishes. The wedding party was led outside, and after picture after picture was taken, the couple was led to the dance floor for their first dance.

The DJ started the song and Charles bowed to his new wife. Taking her in his arms, he began a slow waltz with her as the beginning strings of the song, "I'm Not Lucky, I'm blessed", played.

Slowly they dance around the floor; the moonlight from warm autumn night shining down on them. Bailey looked up into the eyes of her husband when suddenly something caught her eye over near the back of the property. When Charles twirled her, she faced the forest, and there, near the edge was a spot of misty fog, lingering for a moment longer than forest mist should. Warmly she smiled, said a silent prayer, and blew a kiss to the forest; the beautiful forest that had brought her solace, a family, and a love she would cherish until she would one day join that mist. One day, but not any day soon.

As always, to my Readers:

Thank you for going on this journey with me

and allowing me to leave a piece

of my voice on this earth

to share with all.

Miracles and Blessings to you all.

Other works by this Author:

Stories for the Heart and Soul: A Collection of Poetry and Prose

Available at BarnesandNoble.com

And Amazon.com

Made in the USA
Middletown, DE
18 January 2019